Romance in the Stone

Emily Hussey

A collection of six short stories, inspired by gemstones.

***

Warrior Woman
Capture the Moment
In the Cards
The Letters
Change of Heart
Wild Card

"In the Cards" was first published in *Sunstone*, Little Gems Short Story Anthology, 2016, Romance Writers of Australia Inc.
"The Letters" was first published in *Tiger's Eye,* Little Gems Short Story Anthology, 2019, Romance Writers of Australia Inc.
"Wild Cards" was first published in *The Love Hexperts*, 2024

Cover Image: Rawpixel, Unsplash

ISBN 978-1-7640472-1-0

Published by Winsome Books 2025
Adelaide, South Australia

Contents

Foreword

The stories in this collection are small vignettes, each referring in some small way to a gemstone. Some are more obvious than others.

Warrior Woman
She might have been a Qing Dynasty princess. Whatever, the jade statue of a warrior woman was beautiful. Megan discovered more than local history when rain drove her into the museum and into the company of a very intriguing man.

Capture the Moment
A house-sitting cat-walker is disturbed at night by an intruder. He could hardly complain about injuries after giving her such a fright. Still, she didn't expect him to shoot her.

In the Cards
Who knows what the future holds? Rosie was sceptical about the tarot reading. Sometimes, events unfold in the way you least expect. Nearly being run over for a start.

The Letters

Jacinta's aunt left her more than a cottage; she left the clues to a decades-old romance for her to unravel. Solving the mystery brought unexpected results.

Change of Heart

When Scully thought camel wrangling in Australia might make a nice change from running his craft brewery in Ireland, he couldn't have been more mistaken. Best not to get on the wrong side of an aggressive bull camel.

Wild Card

At Coven Fest, gifted seer Gemma reveals a haunting truth to sceptical Saxon—one that no one else could know—and senses he's the soulmate fate has chosen for her. As dark forces close in, her powers and a little magical interference may be the only things that can save him—and bind them together forever.

Emily Hussey
emily@emilyhussey.com.au

Emily Hussey

Warrior Woman

"BASTARD. HE'S OFF the Christmas card list." Megan muttered to herself checking her watch for the umpteenth time. The hands had barely moved since she'd last looked. He wasn't coming. The light misting of rain which had left a glistening on the park morphed into a drenching torrent. She didn't wait any longer. The museum beckoned from across the road. By the time she ran up the steps and skidded through the entrance, she was uncomfortably wet. At least it was dry inside and what else was she going to do?

She by-passed the displays of stuffed animals and other samples of natural history. The shrill voices of school children emanated from those galleries. The thought of that chaos made her shudder. She needed the tranquillity provided by the halls of cultural history.

The display case featuring artefacts of Asian antiquity caught her eye. The red silk slippers, intricately embroidered, were a work of art. There were bowls from various dynasties, their patterns telling a story of the times. Then, there was the figurine. Sculptured from jade, the warrior woman sat on a rosewood base. Megan peered at

3

the intricate carving, wondering how the artisan had created such detailed and delicate work.

"Beautiful, isn't it?"

Megan glanced around in surprise. Was he speaking to her? In the absence of anyone else in the vicinity, it seemed he was. The man was clean-shaven and in a well-cut suit. The shirt he wore in duck-egg blue accented the blue of his eyes. Everything about him spoke of class. She was conscious of her hair settling in a post-rain frizz, and knew she must look as bedraggled as she felt.

"It's intriguing," she offered. "I was admiring the workmanship. It's quite beautiful and technically brilliant. According to the description, it's from the Qing Dynasty and was donated recently."

"That's true. I dropped in to see it in its new home."

"Were you the benefactor?"

She considered the man beside her. She'd thought philanthropists were of advanced years and super rich. Perhaps he was well off, but he looked to be only a few years older than herself. He exuded an air of confidence and authority.

"It belonged to my father. I'm sorting out his estate. I love this woman, but she's too valuable to keep in my apartment. Everyone should have the opportunity to appreciate her, not only me."

"I'm impressed. That's very benevolent of you."

He shrugged. "It was practical. I'm pleased to see she looks at home here."

"If you stand by the display case, I'll take your photo together with the figurine. Then you'll have a record for posterity. I'll email it to you."

He looked surprised but stood where she directed. She also took some separate photos of the warrior woman, checking they were in focus before putting her phone away.

"Where should I send them? They aren't professional quality but they'll be a good memento."

The corner of his mouth twitched as he handed her his business card. Megan watched the movement of those well-formed lips, and wondered what they would feel like pressed against hers. Would he taste as yummy as he looked? She almost missed what he said.

"I'm Simon, by the way. The address on my card will reach me. As a thank you, why don't you join me for coffee? There's a café in the basement."

Megan skimmed the card, taking in the key detail. *Simon Morley – Dealer in Antiquities*. The email address was listed below with his mobile number. Glancing back at him, it was an easy decision. She relegated her previous engagement to irrelevant history.

"Sure—I can look at Asian antiquities any time. I'd love to."

Seated at the table in the café, she looked at the card again.

"It says here you're a dealer in Antiquities. So, you buy and sell antiques? Do you have a shop? Why didn't you sell the figurine if you didn't want it anymore? There would be lots of buyers for such a beautiful piece of jade."

He regarded her for a moment before responding. She was aware of the intensity of his gaze, drawing her into his orbit.

"In answer to your last question, there were a couple of reasons. It seemed tacky to sell off an item like this. I was my father's only heir, so the decision rested with me. It's an important piece historically, and I felt the warrior woman belonged in a location where more people could see and appreciate her."

The coffee arrived, and he paused while the cups were set on the table.

"I don't have a shop, only a website. I source items that I know will be interesting to my clients, and sometimes by specific request. I hold minimal stock; it's easier that way."

He sipped his coffee.

"What about you; what brought you to the museum?"

She wasn't going to tell him about the dating disaster. She would seem such a loser.

"I sought shelter from the rain, hence the drowned rat simulation. I'm a research historian. I'm always keen to see what's on display in the cultural history section, particularly the Asian history. It reflects some of my heritage."

"So that's where you get your beautiful black hair. How did the Asian influence come about?"

"One of my ancestors came to Australia during gold rush in the nineteenth century."

"I assume he settled down here?"

"He did. His wife joined him later, and they established a general store in Ararat. Their descendants intermarried with the local community, so my hair is probably the most distinguishing feature that I've inherited."

Megan tucked errant strands of that hair back behind her ears.

"I still have contact with extended relatives – in fact a distant cousin is my business partner. He's an archaeologist. We provide consultancy services to government agencies and other corporations."

"Fascinating-I'd love to hear more about your work. I have an appointment with a client shortly, but are you free for dinner this evening? You could tell me about it then."

Megan hoped her face didn't show how startled she was. Her day was turning out different than expected, and definitely for the better. Her pause was minimal.

"You're in luck. I've had a cancellation for this evening, so I could join you."

"I hope I'm not a poor substitute. Give me your number and I'll call you later with arrangements."

With details exchanged, he hurried off, leaving Megan to wonder at the turn of events. Life could be full of surprises as she explained later to her cousin, Ryan. They shared an office on the outskirts of the city. Operating costs were low but they still had easy access to their major clients.

"… and he was Mr Suave personified. From what I understood, he's a sort of broker in antiquities. He buys and sells on behalf of clients, usually to order and on commission. It was an amazing piece he donated to the museum. I can show you – I took a photo of it."

She pulled up the photo on her phone and showed it to Ryan. He took the phone from her with a curious look on his face, expanding the picture to magnify the detail.

"Did he say where he got this?"

"Not really, only that it was part of his father's estate. Why?"

"Wait a moment. There's something I need to check."

Ryan came back a short time later holding a photograph.

"Does this look familiar?"

"That's it! That's identical to the figurine in the museum."

"It's a photo of a figurine handed down through the family. An ancestor brought it out from China in the early years. It was stolen from my father some time back."

"It can't be the same one, surely?"

"I don't know, but I might head into the museum to check. If it is, I'd like to know where your friend laid his hands on it. Don't say anything to him until I've checked it out."

When the phone rang a couple of hours later, her heart did a little jig of excitement. The voice on the other end was velvety smooth.

"I've made a booking at a restaurant down by the river for seven this evening. Where should I pick you up?"

Megan hesitated a moment. She didn't know this man. Did she want to disclose her address to him? What if he was caught up in something illegal? On the other hand, there was a vibe about him that was so appealing. She dictated her address, rationalising that at least Ryan knew who she was with.

She'd changed a couple of times before Simon arrived, settling on a simple dress in deep green jersey. It draped softly and fitted snugly. She teamed it with an amber necklace to provide the contrast, and swept her hair back on one side, secured by a tortoiseshell clip.

When she opened the door, she was inwardly delighted to see he was as gorgeous as she remembered, and the smile he gave in greeting seemed genuine.

"Wow! Love that colour on you. It suits. You remind me of the warrior woman. I hope you like Italian," he added.

"I'm easily pleased—in most things anyway."

Megan gave what she hoped was a combination of dazzling yet sophisticated smile as she accompanied him to the car. The evening already showed promise.

They chose an outdoor table where they could view the activity on the river. A smattering of boats sailed past, and pedestrians strolled along the boardwalk. It was peaceful, in spite of the central location. With orders placed, they settled back with a pre-dinner glass of wine.

"Sorry to rush off today. You were telling me earlier you're a research historian."

"That's right. Ryan, my business partner and I, do contract work when new developments are in the planning stages. Alternatively, government agencies might want to improve their knowledge of historical influences in an area."

"So based on your research, previous site uses are acknowledged and possibly preserved?

"That's right. My thesis was on the impact of early Chinese migration to Australia, so you can understand why I was so interested in your figurine. You mentioned it was your father's. Did he travel to China?"

"No, though he was an inveterate collector of fine art and antiquities. It was through him that I developed an interest in my line of work."

"And you buy on behalf of your clients? How do you know where to find the objects they want?"

Simon tapped the side of his nose with a well-manicured finger.

"Trade secret. If I told you my sources, I'd have to kill you."

Seeing her astonished look, he laughed.

"Only joking. Those of us in the industry guard our sources jealously. Over the years I've built up a network of contacts around the world, and if I'm asked to source a particular item, I'll have a general idea who to approach. Often people contact me when they have something they would like to sell. I enjoy matching the right object with the right people. I'll also bid at auctions for clients who wish to preserve their anonymity."

"That sounds more fun than operating from an antique store. I can see why you'd enjoy it."

Megan found the whole concept fascinating, almost as much as the man himself. At that moment, his phone rang. With a frown of annoyance, he glanced at the screen.

"Sorry, I should have turned it off but I need to take this call. Do you mind if I answer it?"

He left the table and moved a couple of metres to one side. The conversation was just audible, although Megan wasn't trying to listen.

"This isn't a convenient time, Rupert. How much is there? Can't *you* store them? We need to keep this quiet."

Megan froze. What could he be talking about? Surely not stolen goods? She thought of her earlier conversation with Ryan. Perhaps some of those industry sources were not above board. She realised he was terminating the call and casually looked towards the river, as though absorbed in the antics of the ducks.

"Sorry about that," he said as he returned to the table. "That's one of the problems with working the way I do – calls can come in at any time."

Their meals arrived at that point, and there was little opportunity to find out what the phone call might have been about. The conversation moved to safer ground, exploring mutual interests and filling in details about their lives to date. Megan noticed however whenever she asked Simon a question about his life, he gave a general answer and then turned it around to a question about her.

"You must travel a lot for your business, Simon. Do you travel to Asia?

"Sometimes. Tell me about *your* travels. Have you ever been to China? Have you researched your ancestral roots?"

He was charming and attentive, and gave Megan the impression of being genuinely interested in her life and experiences. She enjoyed being the focus of attention. When he finally drove her home, he walked her to her door and kissed her, his lips exploring at first before claiming hers with a sense of proprietorship that seemed natural.

Mm. Megan liked the way he tasted. So that's what it's like. I'll take more of that. She slid her arms around his body and beneath his jacket. She could feel his firm, muscular back. This man had distinct possibilities.

When he finally broke away, they were both left breathless, staring at each other with a bruised hunger.

"Megan, I'd better go while I can. I don't want to rush this. I want to take my time getting to know you and to savour every moment. I'll call you tomorrow, if that's all right?"

Then he was gone. Entering her apartment, Megan shut the front door and leaned against it, taking stock of events. It had been an unexpected day, from beginning to end. What was next?

***

"It's the same figurine. This is definitely the one stolen from my father."

Ryan's tone was flat. "I need to have words with this new friend of yours."

"Ryan, I don't think we should rush this. Can you leave it with me for a while?"

He didn't look happy at this request, but acquiesced. That left Megan with a problem—how to raise it with

Simon. When he did call, it was with an invitation causing her breath to quicken.

"I've got to see a contact in Ballarat on Saturday. Why don't you come too? If we leave early we could have a pub lunch and make a day of it – maybe trawl through some regional galleries as well."

The prospect of a whole day in his company was too good to turn down. She would also have the opportunity to find out the answers to those questions that bothered her.

"You've won me; I'd love to go."

It was a beautiful day full of promise when Simon knocked on her door with a greeting kiss.

"Morning, Sunshine."

"Is that a reflection of my yellow blouse, or my sunny disposition?"

"Bit of both. Whatever. You'll brighten up what would otherwise be a mundane trip. I'll need to see Rupert first, but otherwise the day is ours."

"This Rupert", she queried nonchalantly when they were on their way, "is he a dealer?"

"Wheeler dealer, more like. In this instance some World War I memorabilia has come into his hands, including letters and a diary. He's moving business premises so I'll keep them safe for now. It's highly sought-after material. Museums and collectors will be after this lot."

"Wow—and historians too. Do you think I might take a look?"

"For the right woman, I'm sure that might be possible. Not in the pub though. It would be better in a controlled environment, where we can handle the material appropriately."

"Absolutely. I'll even contribute some historical research, if you like."

He turned his head to smile at her. "This has the makings of a great partnership. That would be fantastic."

They arrived late morning. It was definitely lunchtime by the time they completed transactions with Rupert. A pub overlooking Lake Wendouree beckoned. Megan was more hungry than she cared to admit, and the view was convivial, to say nothing of the company. It was time though to raise *that* topic. She could do it while they were waiting for their meals.

"Tell me more about the jade figurine. How did your father come to own it? Was he a dealer as well?"

Simon laughed.

"Far from it. He was a gambler. Our fortunes rose and fell according to his luck with cards. He scored the figurine in payment for a gambling debt when the loser was skint. My father had a winning streak after that and attributed it to the 'Lucky Lady' as he called her. He wouldn't sell it, thinking if he did, his luck would run out."

"The loser must have been devastated." *That was the understatement of the day.* Her eyes widened at the thought and the implications.

"I believe so. The jade had been in his family for generations. He couldn't tell them what he'd done. He would have lost so much face. That's also one of the reasons I donated it" He shrugged his shoulders with an open-handed gesture. "I've no idea who this man was. It was a long time ago and I was never told his name, but it seems wrong to hold onto an item which has strong sentimental value for another family. At least now, they might see it again."

Megan sipped her drink, wondering what she could tell Ryan. That discussion required sensitivity. She would deal with that later. Right now, there were other things to think about. Like the man sitting opposite. The relief on discovering he was not a thief was immense. Already, the day seemed sunnier. She was spending the day with someone who gave every indication of being a person of integrity. Best of all, he was gorgeous.

Simon reached across the table and took her hand. "I have to agree with my father—it *was* lucky jade. It's through the figurine I met you."

Megan smiled, returning his gaze. Mentally, she re-wrote her Christmas card list for the second time. Never had being stood up turned out so well.

Capture the Moment

THE DOOR SLAMMED behind her as Ellie threw the keys in the direction of the onyx ashtray on the hall table. Princess Leila was voicing her displeasure at confinement and Ellie's first priority was to release her from captivity. The feline stalked from the carrier with one last indignant yowl and a flick of her tail. She pointedly refused to look in Ellie's direction.

It was in the contract so like it or not, Ellie and Princess Leila made their way to the local park, her highness making that journey in a padded carrier. Once inside the gates, Ellie opened the carrier, and Leila was free to explore, and sniff and roll in the grass. She explored on the end of a scarlet leash that contrasted with her coffee cream coat.

Leila was not impressed. In the apartment, she resisted going into the carrier and when it was opened in the park, she had to be dragged out, hissing and spitting. Janey Jefferson, owner of both Princess Leila and the apartment decreed that it was not good for anyone to be shut up inside for too long. Her feline should visit the park daily unless it was raining.

Ellie acknowledged that it gave her an opportunity that most people could only dream about. She had penthouse accommodation in the centre of the city, a cleaner who came twice a week and a cute little Mercedes Hatch at her disposal. All this in return for the care of Her Highness and ensuring the house orchids continued to bloom. In two days Janey would be home from her latest cruise and then it would be back to the real world – or wherever House-sitters-R-Us sent her next.

She wasn't sure what woke her. Probably that damn cat. A true princess, its demands were not limited to daylight hours. Ellie kept her eyes shut on the theory that if she didn't open them, she wasn't properly awake and could slide back into sleep.

This time the noise was both definite and distinct. Ellie froze. It was in the apartment. Opening her eyes, she could discern the shape of the cat on the end of her bed. A quick glance at the clock revealed that it was 1:30 am. What to do? The building concierge would have gone home long ago and she had left her phone on the dining table. She could feel her heart thumping, almost convinced that she heard it as well.

Easing out of the bed, Ellie padded to the door, opening it a crack. A light was on in the kitchen. What a nerve – not only was there an intruder, but he or she was cheeky enough to switch on the lights as well. If she crept down the hall, maybe she could slip out the door to the apartment and summons help. Thank goodness for plush pile carpet.

She had almost reached the door when she heard a muttered

"What the…?"

Spinning round, she took in the dark shape of a man silhouetted between her and the kitchen light. He was wearing a hooded top and carrying a duffle bag. Without stopping to think, she grabbed the first thing to hand and threw it at him. It was the onyx ashtray from the hall table. It connected with a satisfying whack. She'd never been very good at ball sports. She lunged for the door handle. Locked. Where were the keys? It was then she remembered they had been in the ashtray when she'd picked it up and flung it. They must be on the floor, somewhere near the intruder.

She backed up against the door and seized an umbrella from the adjacent stand. At least she could go down fighting. The man hunched over holding his head. Straightening up, he looked in her direction and made as if to move towards her. She raised the umbrella and channelled her most ferocious look – the one she reserved for dogs that came too close to her and Princess Leila in the park.

"Don't come any closer!"

"Do I look stupid? You're clearly dangerous. Before I call the police, would you mind telling me what you are doing here?"

"Why should *you* call you police? You're the intruder."

"I live here and you sure as hell don't. You've got thirty seconds before I start dialling. Don't move from there – I'm switching on the light."

The man in front of her was unshaven and looked as though a haircut was overdue. His eyes were red-rimmed and bleary, but not as red as the trickle of blood that made its way down the side of his face. A sharp corner of the ashtray must have caught him on the temple. The way that he was clutching at his head indicated that it was giving him some grief. In his other hand, he held a phone.

"Start talking. Are you squatting or what? Who let you in?"

"Squatting," she spluttered. "I'm the house sitter. I'm looking after the apartment for the owner and that isn't you. What are you doing here, sneaking around in the middle of the night like the thief that you obviously are?"

"I'm Janey Jefferson's nephew and I live here."

"No you don't. You weren't mentioned in the contract and if you lived here, I would have noticed by now."

"I travel—a lot. I use this as a base when I'm back in town but I've returned earlier than scheduled. I've been incommunicado but I expected Janey to be here."

"She's back in a couple of days." Ellie lowered the umbrella but kept a firm grip on it. She still wasn't totally convinced. At that point, a yawning Leila strolled into the room and with a delicate yowl of greeting, rubbed against the intruder's legs.

"Leila, old girl; at least somebody's pleased to see me."

Ellie stared. The animal had rarely acknowledged her existence, let alone shown any affection. Maybe he was telling the truth.

"Umm—you're bleeding."

"I wonder why that is? I know – some near-naked woman chose to assault me in the middle of the night in my own home."

It was only then Ellie remembered what she was wearing. A silky lace trim cami and short set that left little to the imagination, particularly as her nipples had reacted predictably to the cool of the night. She threw an arm across her breasts, retreating a step at the same time. She couldn't turn around. The back view was more lace than silk. She wasn't exactly dressed for receiving visitors.

"Stay there. I'll be back in a moment."

Ellie backed out of the room. When it was safe to do so, she turned and dashed for the safety of her bedroom, shutting and locking the door behind her. She leant against it, willing her heart to slow down to a normal pace. She recalled now that there had been mention of a relative of Janey's but nothing specific and certainly nothing about him returning while she was in residence. There were two other bedrooms in the apartment. She'd not investigated them but one was presumably his. Now she had injured him. This could mean trouble. Would House-sitters-R-Us give her another job after this?

She pulled on jeans and a t-shirt and padded back to the kitchen. He was still there, blotting at his head with wads of paper towel.

"Sit down. I'll tape it up for you."

"I don't think I want you to touch me again, thank you very much."

"Don't be so silly," Ellie snapped. "If I'd known to expect you I wouldn't have had to throw anything at you."

"So it's my fault that you damn near split my head in two?" He sounded unimpressed.

"Shut up and sit down and I'll clean it up. Or not. It's up to you. You can bleed all over yourself if you want – just don't get any blood on the floor."

"A true Florence Nightingale" he muttered, but he sat down. Ellie cleaned the wound and taped it closed. He might have a bit of a scar but it should heal without needing stitches. With all the blood it looked worse than it was. He might have a sore head for a while though.

"At least the ashtray didn't break," she remarked as she finished her ministrations. "I guess your head isn't so hard after all. Breakages are always an embarrassment."

"Are you referring to my head or to the ashtray?"

"Well, both I guess but at least your head will heal. Breakages put a black mark on your record with the company."

"You don't say! You do realise this particular onyx item is a family heirloom? It belonged to my uncle in his smoking days and I think belonged to his father before him."

He sounded aggrieved and Ellie felt a pang of embarrassment.

"Would you like some paracetamol? You may have a bit of a headache. Sorry, by the way. If I'd known who you were, I wouldn't have hit you. I think you'll live. Unless you need anything else and if it's okay with you, I'm going back to bed. I assume you know the way to your room."

The only response she got was a grunt and a look that indicated all was not forgiven. She beat a tactful retreat.

There was no sign of him when she got up the next morning. Princess Leila wasn't around either. Ellie assumed the cat must have bedded down with the human she preferred. She made a pot of coffee and tidied up a bit in anticipation of the cleaner's arrival. Ellie put out a mug for Lizzie as well, knowing that the cleaner appreciated a coffee at the start of her day.

"Luke's back you say? I love looking at his work. His aunt will be so pleased to see him. She misses him when he's not here."

"Work? What sort of work?" Ellie asked.

"Have a look in the bookcase. He's a photographer and publishes a lot of books. His aunt has them all. Can't stay here chatting; I must get on with the vacuuming. That cat leaves hair everywhere."

Ellie soon found the books. She'd noticed them before when looking for something to read but hadn't actually pulled them off the shelf. She pulled one out now and sat down to go through it in detail. It was evident that Luke Jefferson specialised in environmental photography. A foreword to the book by a well-known environmental champion praised the work Luke did in bringing the loss of natural habitats to public attention. The photos were intimate in their detail. It was as though the photographer was flying with eagles or swimming beneath the oceans. How did he manage to get those shots?

22

"Looking at something interesting?"

Ellie hadn't heard him enter the room, so taken was she with the images and the explanations that accompanied them. Looking up, for the first time she was able to get a good look at the man. He was actually more attractive than the photo on the back of the book. Now clean-shaven and fresh out of the shower, his blue eyes contrasted with the sort of tan indicating he spent time outdoors. His white t-shirt outlined his form neatly enough to allow an appreciation of the body beneath. Her eyes settled on the medical tape on his forehead.

"Umm—did you sleep okay? The cleaner filled me in a bit on the sort of work you do. It's impressive. You must get to some interesting parts of the world."

"It was an unsettled sleep. Might have had something to do with a thumping headache. And yes, I do get to see some interesting parts of the world. I've just returned from an assignment in Antarctica."

"Look I'm sorry about your head. If I'd known you were coming, I would have laid out the welcome mat."

"That could have been a more interesting home-coming, especially in that outfit."

"In your dreams."

The withering look was not encouraging. She wondered if she should move within reach of the ashtray again. At the same time, a small part of her wondered what it would have been like, if circumstances has been different. Welcoming home a man who had spent weeks at the South Pole would have been quite a memorable experience. She inwardly blushed and banished the thought.

As if he read her mind, he grinned and moved instead to refill his coffee.

"Actually, I'd forgotten Aunt Janey was going to be away. There was a serious bout of rotavirus in the camp. The medical superintendent decreed that we should return early rather than infect the next expedition that was due to arrive. I'd got the pictures I needed anyway so it was fine by me."

Ellie indicated the book. "If these pictures are anything to go by, I look forward to seeing the latest efforts. Are you publishing another book?"

"Maybe. It was a project with the Climate Change Commission, recording the changes occurring in Antarctica with the increase in global warming. There are still decisions to be made on how the pictures will be used. If that coffee's still hot, I wouldn't mind a cup."

"I'll make a fresh pot. Then I'd better take Princess Leila for her morning walk."

His mouth twitched. "That'll be fun. Perhaps I'll come too and bring my camera."

"No way! I'm not appearing in any future publications, walking a cat in the park. That's fifteen minutes of fame I don't need."

She should have saved her breath. Not only did Luke accompany them, but he brought his backpack full of equipment. At his direction, Leila entered her carrier without a single hiss or snarled objection. *He has a way of handling the animal. I wonder if he manages all females like that?* There appeared to be a trusting relationship between the two. Ellie wasn't sure whether to be relieved or jealous.

Leila performed as one would expect of a princess – one who is used to attention and knows how to ignore the camera. She sat serenely, chased butterflies, sniffed flowers and balanced on park sculptures. Luke allowed Ellie to look at the photos via image playback.

"This cat could have her own Instagram account," she said. "She's sure to get thousands of followers. A video of her walking on the leash would be a hit on YouTube. I can easily organise an account for her. I've set up a few for other people. She could become famous."

Luke laughed. "As far as Leila is concerned, she already is."

Scrolling back further, Ellie caught her breath. It wasn't only the feline whose image had been captured. There were photos of her - walking with Leila, laughing at something off camera, and balancing on a fence railing behind the cat. She saw herself in a new light. They were candid images that captured spontaneous emotion and she looked as though she hadn't a care in the world; which of course she hadn't—not really.

"I didn't know you were taking these."

"You weren't supposed to."

"What are you intending to do with them?"

"I haven't decided. Perhaps I can start a new Instagram Account—lady and the cat series, a follow on from 'lady in flimsy night attire attacks man' series."

She blushed. "You didn't take any?"

"No, but I wish I had. I was somewhat incapacitated in case you hadn't noticed."

"It doesn't seem to have had any long term effects," Ellie remarked dryly. Anyway, I wasn't attacking you. I was defending myself."

"I hadn't laid a finger on you!"

"No, but you could have. I wasn't going to take the chance. At least there's nothing wrong with my reflexes, and I did say sorry." She hoped that she looked contrite. If he made an official complaint, that would be the end of her house-sitting career.

He looked at her speculatively. "You know my aunt is going to ask what happened to my head."

"You won't say I threw the ashtray at you, will you? If she puts in a bad report to House-sitters –R-Us, I'll never get another placement. They're a bit funny about that sort of thing."

"And so they should be. Can't have clients and their families being assaulted. I think it's time we took Princess Leila home, don't you? After that, we could talk about compensation for a broken head and what my silence is worth."

It was a warm day, but a chill washed over Elli. What could he mean? She fretted all the way back to the apartment and only half listened as he recounted the highlights of his journey back from Antarctica. She stole quick glances at his profile as they walked, but there was nothing to be discerned from his demeanour. There was a solid presence about the man and she liked what she saw. Under different circumstances, she might be tempted to do something about that. Right now though, any advances might be misconstrued as though she were trying to buy her way out of the situation by non-financial means.

"I've been thinking," Luke said. He shut the apartment door, wincing slightly as his eyes encountered the onyx ashtray, back on the hall table. "I know we were joking about social media but perhaps I could focus more on this area as a way of getting my message across. Climate change isn't always sexy, but you could help me address that. I'm in control behind a camera but I've no patience for social media."

"And if I help you, you won't report me to House-sitters-R-Us?"

He laughed. "You didn't seriously think that I would, do you? What sort of person do you think I am?"

"The sort of person who takes photos of women when they're not looking."

"With the right subject, it's an automatic response like a few others I could name. I've got to capture the moment." He paused before continuing. "Of course, I do have an ulterior motive with my suggestion."

Ellie turned to face him. There was a hint of a smile beneath a tantalisingly enigmatic look.

"And that is?"

"If you're my social media manager, I won't have to make excuses to keep seeing you."

"You want to see me again?" She caught her breath, not quite sure what she was hearing.

"The image of you dressed in that amazing lace concoction wielding an umbrella like a modern-day

Boadicea was extraordinary. How could I resist a vision like that?"

Her heart did a little happy dance. She gave him a low-lidded come-hither look. "We might come to a mutually acceptable arrangement."

Luke wasn't the only one who found certain visions appealing. Not that she imagined him in silk and lace but there were other tantalizing options. Even Leila was purring.

Emily Hussey

In the Cards

"DO YOU HAVE specific questions Rosie, or do you want a review of the year ahead?"

Rosie thought for a while. She did want to know if new work opportunities were coming her way, but it would be good to have a broad picture.

"A review of the year please."

Xaveria handed her the deck of cards. "Concentrate on the coming year and shuffle the deck. Clear your head of mindless chatter; only focus on the year ahead."

Rosie did as instructed. She shut her eyes to focus on positive energy and abundant thoughts. After the last miserable year, she could do with both. She returned the deck to Xaveria, who dealt seven cards from the top, and spread them out in a semi-circle.

"Interesting, very interesting," the woman intoned.

"What do you see? Nothing bad I hope."

"Patience young lady, patience." Xaveria tapped the first card. 'Finance… you've been spending a bit lately and this is the year of consolidation. You need to put a proper savings plan into action."

She must have been talking to my parents. I didn't come here for a lecture on my spending habits.

"Health… hmm I see an issue with your knees, or is it ankles? Do you play sport? No? Skiing perhaps? There could be a problem in the next couple of months. Work… some changes ahead. Travel… I see you taking an unexpected journey. Family… joyful news - another baby—any history of twins in your family?"

"Heavens; I don't think so. I'm not sure whether to relay that to my sister or not. She already has two little boys under three. It must be her because it wouldn't be me!"

Xaveria smiled briefly and continued. "Love; some fascinating prospects on the horizon. I see a man who has an interest in Central America. The last card indicates the highlights of the year. There could be challenges early on and you will be called upon to support others. This will bring you much satisfaction. You will move house in the second half of the year, possibly around September."

"Your lucky number is four, and your protective gemstone is moonstone. Keep it close to you and it will shield you from negative energies. The aura I perceive about you is orange, and this is the colour of adventure and social communication. You have an interesting year ahead."

There was more but Rosie had forgotten most of it by the time she had paid her money and taken her leave. Well that was a waste of time, she thought as she made her way back up the high street. *Nothing specific about anything really. Twins—wouldn't that be a hoot, and orange—she's got to be kidding.*

Rosie by name, but not by colouring. Her hair was a deep burnished carrot, and orange was a colour she avoided like the plague. She preferred blues and greens as a cooling antidote to the fiery thatch. She wandered back to where she had secured her bike and unlocked the chain. It was a beautiful day, and she had opted for the bike over the car. The Saturday morning shoppers were out in force, and car parks were at a premium. Rosie felt rather smug as she zoomed along the bike lane. No parking problems for her.

With little warning, the driver of a car parked ahead opened a door in her path. Rosie hit the brake but with insufficient time to stop, careened into the open door. The next thing she knew, she and the bike were a tangled heap in the middle of the road as an approaching SUV bore down on her. She squeezed her eyes shut, knowing that this was it. Almost. There was a squeal of brakes and a smell of rubber. A door slammed. She felt the bike being lifted from her legs. A child wailed in the background, or was it her?

"Are you hurt?"

She opened her eyes. Was she hurt? Yes, no, maybe. She wasn't sure of anything. A face loomed over her. It was the man who had asked the question.

"Take it easy. Can you wriggle your toes? Tell me where it hurts."

"I'm okay. I'm fine, I think. Just a little winded. It was all so quick."

"I'm so sorry," the owner of the parked car babbled. "The kids distracted me, and I didn't look before opening the door. I'll pay if there's any damage to the bike." The woman was distraught.

"Let's get her off the road first and we'll sort out the details later."

It was the man again.

"Put your arm around my neck and I'll help you up."

Rosie was aware of his strength as he hoisted her into an upright position. Lucky he still had a firm grip on her. When she tried to take a step, a sharp pain shot through her knee, and she sagged against him.

"Right. It's a doctor for you." He picked her up as though she were no heavier than a bag of grocery shopping, and deposited her on a park bench. While she sat there and exchanged details with the woman from the parked car, The man dragged her bike off the road.

"I'll secure your bike for now and then take you down to the local clinic. I'm Jared, by the way."

Rosie looked at him properly for the first time. He was not conventionally handsome but there was a rugged appeal about him. She noted the aquiline nose and well-formed lips that now had a hint of a smile. One eyebrow rose, as though to ask, "Well, do I pass?" She averted her eyes. She hadn't meant to stare.

"I'm Rosie. Thanks for not running me over."

"Well, it could have been messy, and the bike might have scratched my car."

Rosie would have laughed if her knee wasn't hurting so much. Jared secured her bike and assisted her into the front seat of his SUV. When they arrived at the clinic, he retrieved a wheelchair from inside. Helping Rosie into it, he pushed her into the reception area.

"Look, you don't have to stay," she said. "I've already messed up your morning. It might be a while before the doctor sees me and I can get a taxi home after that."

"It's no problem. I'll make a couple of calls to re-arrange my day. I'll make myself comfy with ancient copies of Readers' Digest and Golfing Australia. Can I get you a magazine?"

In the end, they didn't have to wait long. A medical inspection decreed nothing was broken, but she had probably a torn ligament in the knee joint. The doctor strapped it up, and delivered Rosie back to the waiting room. He gave her some pain killers with instructions to rest up and apply a cold pack every three to four hours.

"She's not to put any stress on that knee," the doctor advised Jared. "You'll have to take care of her and make sure that she rests. Bring her back in three days so we can review progress. We'll decide then if she needs any further treatment. She'll benefit later from some physiotherapy to regain full mobility in that knee."

"I'll take excellent care of her, Doctor. Thank you."

"Oh, but…"

"Now Rosie, no buts. You heard what the doctor said. Time to get you home."

"Why did you let him think that we're a couple?" she queried as he pushed the wheelchair back to the car park. "You don't have to take me home. I can get a taxi as I said before."

"It was too much effort to explain, and it's easier for you to get into my car than a taxi. You gave me such a fright today. I keep seeing you there lying in front of my wheels. For one horrible moment, I didn't think that I would be able to stop in time."

"Nor did I actually. It wasn't your fault though so you don't have to take responsibility for me."

"Stop quibbling and tell me where you live. I'll drop you off, see you to your door and then I'll go. I promise."

Rosie wondered if she should snap a photo of his car number plate with her phone and email it to a friend. but then felt rather silly. It wasn't as if he'd done anything to make her mistrust him. Quite the opposite in fact and being honest, she'd like to get to know him better. If she wasn't in so much pain, she would have thought about how to achieve that. Right now, all she wanted to do was get home, take her pain relief and lie down for a while.

"Thank you. That's very kind." She gave Jared her address and he delivered her to the front door. Then he took the key from her hands, unlocked the door and assisted her inside.

"Where's the kitchen? I'll get you a glass of water for those tablets and you can lie down. Is there anyone to look in on you?"

"Yes, of course. I'll give my family a call. Thank you so much Jared. I appreciate your help. It will be good to lie down for a while though."

***

Rosie didn't feel rested the following day. Her mother had come over the previous evening and brought an ice pack and some soup for a light meal. It was difficult to get comfortable in bed, and she had spent a restless night. Thoughts of the near miss when she was lying on the road kept running through her mind, and that didn't help either.

She still wasn't feeling her best when there was a knock at the door late morning. With difficulty, she limped to answer it. Jared stood there, and her bike was leaning against the wall.

"So how are you feeling today? I put my bike rack on and picked the bike up from where we left it. The key to the lock was still in my car, so I thought I'd bring the bike home for you. Where should I put it? I don't want to leave it there in full view of the street."

"Umm–can you put it around the back? The side gate isn't locked. I'll open the back door for you."

Rosie grabbed a brush and dragged some order through her hair as she hobbled to the back door. She hadn't expected a visitor, and in particular not Jared. Opening the door, she saw he had already put her bike under cover. He stood, looking at it critically.

"It's not too bad but the front wheel has a slight buckle. You'll need to take it to a bike mechanic before you go riding again. I can recommend someone good if you don't have one. He keeps my wheels in good condition."

"So you ride a bike too? Do come in – would you like a cup of coffee?"

"Yes, I ride and yes, I'd love a cup of coffee. When you're mobile again, we can always do a day trip along

Linear Park if you're up for it? You sit down and I'll make the coffee. How are you feeling?"

It was strange to see a man making himself at home in her kitchen. Rosie perched on a stool at the breakfast bar, directing Jared where to find the cups and coffee. He seemed quite at ease, delivering the two steaming cups before pulling up a stool beside her.

It gave her a moment in which to observe him without seeming to stare. Riding his bike was not his only exercise, for he looked fit and his clothes sat comfortably on his frame. It was a nice compact derriere that sat inside his jeans. To her surprise, he was wearing a small diamond ear stud, or at least she assumed that it was diamond. Could have been synthetic but somehow, he didn't appear a synthetic type of guy. Getting to know him better could be interesting.

"Before I forget, here's the key to your bike lock. It's so tiny; it's easy to overlook it."

"Don't I know it. I'm forever misplacing it. Thanks for bringing the bike back. To be honest, I'd forgotten about it. I'm tied to the house for now anyway so I couldn't have picked it up."

"Do you need to go anywhere?"

"No--lucky it's a Sunday. My mother's picking up some crutches for me from the clinic and I've arranged a lift to work tomorrow. I should be I'll be fine through the week. For today though, I'm stuck here and happy to take it easy."

"Well the doctor did say to rest up and keep off your feet. I don't want to intrude on you now. You rest this afternoon, but I've a suggestion. I could come back this evening with some take-away. That will save you worrying about making a meal."

"Jared, you've done enough for me already. I don't expect you to feed me as well."

"I can't imagine you hobbling around the kitchen this evening, crutches or not. I can see by your face that you should be lying down again. How about we move to the living room and you can lie down on your couch."

Jared carried their coffees and Rosie manoeuvred herself to the living room. It *was* a relief to lie down again. Jared made sure that the television remote was in easy reach and that she had a couple of books nearby. Rosie had a stack of library books sitting on a shelf, and for a while they discussed reading preferences.

"You look like you could use some quiet time. I'll leave you to it, and I'll see you later." He stood up, picking up the cups to take back to the kitchen.

"I might snooze for a while,' Rosie said. 'I didn't sleep so well last night so a siesta would be good."

They made arrangements about the time he would return, and her food preferences. Jared departed leaving Rosie to her thoughts. Scattered thoughts they were too. She was half bemused at the turn of events that had introduced her to Jared, and half unsure of where things might be heading. On top of that, where did she want them to head? Too many questions. She snoozed instead.

By the time Jared returned, Rosie had showered and changed. She managed to manoeuvre her way around the house with the crutches her mother had delivered. It was slow progress, but she had managed to put some wine in the fridge to chill, and set the table. He arrived exactly when he said he would.

"Well you've got a bit more colour in your cheeks now. Your nap must have done you good. Show me the plates and I'll sort this food out."

"I can do that," Rosie protested. "It's only my knee that's the problem. The rest of me's fine."

"I've noticed,' he said, giving her a glance imbued with meaning. 'The rest of you is *more* than fine. No point in undoing the good work you've done today though. Sit down and I'll bring it all over. I can see that the table is ready so you've done your bit."

Rosie had to satisfy her need to be hospitable by getting the wine from the fridge, and pouring them each a glass. The meal was relaxed. They each chatted about their work, their families and interests in general. It was part of the 'getting-to-know-you' ritual. Rosie was surprised at how much they had in common. They had both done a bit of travelling and hoped to do some more. Both had learnt rudimentary Italian, and both enjoyed cooking. Flavour of the month for Jared was Mexican, but Rosie was experimenting with Vietnamese.

"I almost forgot," he exclaimed. They had finished the meal, but were still finishing their wine. "I brought you something. Sorry, it's not gift-wrapped.'"

From his pocket, he took a small paper bag. Rosie recognised the logo as being from the gift shop that was next to where they had left her bike the day before.

"I love surprises Jared, but I wasn't expecting a gift. You even brought the meal."

"I know, but I thought this would be useful. Have a look."

Opening the bag, Rosie drew out a key ring. It featured a small orange cabochon set in silver. The colouring was unusual. As she examined it, the stone reacted with flashes of reflected light.

'"It's for that little bike key so that you don't have any problems finding it in the future. It's set with a sunstone.'

"It's beautiful--thank you." Rosie reached across the table to touch his hand. "I can't thank you enough for all the help you've given me."

His eyes met hers across the table, and his smile held the promise of good times to come. Rosie was aware of the butterflies that were starting to dance the fandango in the pit of her stomach.

It was only after he had gone, that Rosie could mentally review the weekend. He left with arrangements made for their next meeting, so that was something to look forward to. Xaveria had been right after all—well almost. She *did* have a problem with her knee; there *were* interesting prospects on the horizon, and it looked like an interesting year ahead. Xaveria made a mistake about the stone. It should have been sunstone, not moonstone and as for twins—no way!

***

Capture the Moment was short-listed for the 2016 Little Gems Award, conducted by the Romance Writers of Australia. It was first published in the anthology printed as a result of that Award.

Emily Hussey

The Letters

THE DOOR NEEDED a shove before it swung inwards, protesting on its hinges. A musty smell greeted Jacinta as she hesitated on the doorstep. An arm reached past her and flicked a light switch. Dim light filled the passage stretching before her. Either Cynthia used low-wattage globes, or this one struggled through a film of dust. Perhaps both.

She blinked uncertainly as dust motes swirled before her eyes. She'd spent summer holidays here as a child, but that was long ago. Where to begin? She was conscious of the clean citrus smell of the man beside her. Soap or cologne? It cut a pleasant contrast to the mustiness.

"Would you like me to stay?" he asked. "I can call the office and tell them to re-schedule today's appointments."

"Thanks, Paul, but I'll be fine. I'll start in one room and systematically work my way through the house. I have the rest of the week to sort the contents."

"Okay, but don't hesitate to call me if you need anything. You might want this."

Taking the key he held out, Jacinta noted the smooth hands and manicured nails. Looking up, she was drawn to his eyes, illuminated from the light streaming through the open door. They were a sort of sea-green shade of blue and quite mesmerizing.

Jacinta—stop staring! She flicked him a smile of thanks and he turned towards the door. He had almost stepped out into the sunshine when he halted and turned back towards her.

"I nearly forgot. Cynthia made a specific bequest." He took a small box from his jacket pocket and held it out "She left this with us, and asked it be given to you." He gave a half-salute of farewell. "I'll leave you to it. I might drop in later to see how you're going."

This time, he did leave. Jacinta stared at the small velvet-covered box. Cynthia hadn't mentioned this. She flipped the lid open and discovered a pair of drop earrings. The bottom stone was a tiger's eye cabochon; above that, two facetted jet beads were suspended in a sterling silver and marcasite setting. The art deco design indicated the era in which the jewelry may have been made.

The earrings were lovely and very unusual. They must have held a special significance for Cynthia. What a pity she hadn't left a letter or something indicating their background or provenance. Closing the lid, Jacinta slipped the box into her bag. Time to get cracking.

She drew back the curtains in the main bedroom, coughing at the resultant cloud of dust. Opening the doors to the wardrobe, she pulled clothes off their hangars and piled them on the bed. Phew! The clothing had been shut up too long. It was all good quality, but nothing she wanted to keep. She systematically folded items and dropped them into rubbish bags. The shoes followed, sensible and comfortable. The top shelf in the wardrobe yielded hats and handbags. They joined the clothes.

A cardboard box about the size of two shoe boxes sat at the back of the shelf. Jacinta stood on tiptoes to reach it, sliding it forwards to where she could grasp it properly. The box tipped over, spilling photos and letters over the floor. Jacinta knelt down, gathering up the papers. Probably it could go straight in the bin. She picked up one photo and looked at it. A group of unknown people sat around a dining table, glasses raised to the camera. Nothing was written on the back. Bin it.

As she dumped the items back in the box, she came across another photo. This time, she did recognise someone. It was Cynthia, and she was with a man; a rather handsome man. The earrings caught her eye. Cynthia wore the tiger's eye earrings.

She turned the photo over. The inscription was written in Cynthia's neat script. *Gerald and myself, New Year's Eve, 1958.* Who was Gerald? Cynthia hadn't married and never talked about her private life. Jacinta rifled through the rest of the box. There were Christmas cards, postcards, and old theatre programs. The letters tied together in violet ribbon caught her eye. Violet had been Cynthia's favourite colour. She pulled one end of the ribbon, releasing the bow. The letters were addressed to Cynthia, and all in the same hand.

To read someone's private letters seemed intrusive, but as sole beneficiary, there was no reason why she shouldn't

read them. Jacinta sank onto the bed and opened the first
letter.

15/10/1958

Dear Cynthia,
Meeting you last week was an unexpected
pleasure. I would never have come to Pt Reilly if
the Hudsons hadn't persuaded me to join them
at their beach house. I was in need of a break
but was not looking for company. Muriel
Hudson is not one to take no for an answer, and
now I have to say I'm glad.
Can I entice you to come up to the city one
weekend? South Pacific has just been released
and is receiving rave reviews. We could go to
dinner and then see the movie. I'm sure the
Hudsons would be delighted to have you as their
houseguest. I'll speak to Muriel.
Kind regards
Gerald Densley

Jacinta slipped the letter back in the envelope. *I
wonder if Cynthia went to the city? Gerald looks rather
nice. Did she see him again?* She glanced at her watch.
There was time to read one more. She opened the next
letter.

04/11/1958

> *Dearest Cynthia,*
>
> *That music still keeps playing in my head. I really enjoyed your company this weekend. As promised, I'll try to come down again before the end of the month. The Hudsons have offered me the use of their cottage any time, provided they don't have alternative arrangements in place. It is only a day since we saw each other, but I am already missing you.*
>
> *Do you think me crazy if I say I think our meeting was destined to happen? I wish we lived closer to each other. Counting the days until we meet again.*
>
> *Yours ever*
> *Gerald*

Wow. Jacinta fanned herself with the letter before placing it back in the envelope. *I wonder what happened to Gerald? Why didn't Cynthia ever mention him?* She didn't have time to ponder the question. There was still so much work to do. She left the box on the bed and dragged the rubbish bags into the passage. The lounge room was the next target.

Cynthia had never exhibited professionally but was an accomplished   artist. Her paintings, mostly seascapes, hung on the walls of the house. Jacinta knew she would keep some of the artwork. Deciding which was the problem.

"Hello? Jacinta?"

Poking her head around the door of the lounge room, her heart jumped to see a figure silhouetted against the open doorway at the end of the passage.

"Feel like some lunch?" Paul held up two lunch bags. "I picked up some salad rolls. I didn't think you'd have any food here." He came down the passage, moving out of profile and into clearer visibility.

"Paul, that's so thoughtful of you. You're right—I haven't done any shopping yet. Come down to the dining room." She pointed to the piles of bagged clothing. "Mind the bags. This stuff's ready for the op shop."

"You've made some headway then."

Looking at the piles, it was stating the obvious. Jacinta didn't tell him about finding the letters. Paul might have acted for Cynthia, but this was a private matter. She cleared a space for them to sit at the table. On impulse, she pulled a couple of plates out of the selection of 'good china' that was kept in the sideboard. The company was welcome after her morning in solitude, except for the memories.

"Did you know my aunt well?" she asked after a while. "I spent a lot of time here when I was a child but as I grew up, the contact was more sporadic, or via email."

"Dad knew her better than I did. He was her solicitor years before I joined the firm." He paused, head on one side as he considered the question. "Besides drafting and updating her will, there wasn't much she required. Occasionally a document had to be witnessed, but nothing major. In recent times, I came here to save her making the trip to the office."

He smiled, an action that lit up his entire face. "I liked her. She always had a cup of tea waiting, and usually cake. She welcomed the chat, I think. She told me a bit about you. I looked forward to finally meeting you."

Jacinta blushed inwardly. *I wish she'd told me about you.* "She must have been lonely. It makes me feel guilty." Visiting her aunt was one of those things she meant to do, but something else always came up. "Probably a lot of her friends had moved on in one way or another."

"She attended the art group each week, but she liked to reminisce about earlier days. My father was a better-informed listener. They knew some of the same people."

There was a moment's silence. Jacinta cleared her throat awkwardly. "I'm sorry to hear about your dad. You must miss him."

"I do, but you know—your aunt, my dad… it's not unexpected but you just hope 'not yet'.

Cup of tea. I should offer him a cup of tea. "Would you like a cuppa? I brought some milk and basic supplies with me."

Paul stood up, brushing crumbs from his suit. "Thanks, but I'd better get back to the office and leave you to your sorting. Do you want me to drop those bags off for you?"

Jacinta brightened. "That would be really helpful. There's not much room in my small car." She grabbed one of the bags as well and followed him outside. "I appreciate all you're doing for me. Can I return the favour and invite you to dinner this evening?" *Did I really say that? I don't know much about him. What if he's not available?*

Paul shut the boot of the car and moved around to stand beside her in the driveway. He momentarily blocked the sun, making her appreciate how tall he was. "That's not necessary. I don't want to put you to any trouble."

"It's no trouble at all. I have to cook for myself so I can easily cook for two. I'll do some shopping later today." She added a persuasive tone to her voice. "I'd love to hear more about Cynthia's stories." *And if she mentioned anything about Gerald.*

"Okay." The smile illuminated his face. "I'd welcome the opportunity to become better acquainted after hearing so much about you. I'll bring the wine. I'll feel bad if I don't contribute something."

Jacinta returned inside after Paul had driven off. She should be focusing on the lounge room, but Gerald's letters drew her back to the bedroom. She told herself she would only read one or two and would then continue sorting. She took the next envelope from the bundle and pulled out the letter.

3/12/1958

My Darling Cynthia
The weekend went so quickly; I hated
leaving you Sunday evening. I have been
thinking about our future options. Spending time
apart is killing me, but the alternative means
either you moving to the city, or me moving
down to Pt Reilly. Darling girl, I know you will
be reluctant to leave your family and I

*understand that. I am reliant on work
opportunities, so whether I can relocate will
depend on securing suitable employment. This is
presuming you would like to see more of me. I
don't want there to be any misunderstandings. If
you don't want me around, please say so. For
myself, I know I have met the woman with whom
I want to play an ongoing role in my life.*

*Don't leave me in suspense. Write to me
soon. With all my love,*
Gerald

It was frustrating to only have access to Gerald's words. What was Cynthia's response? Did she feel the same? Jacinta refolded the letter and picked out their photo again from the box. She looked at them both with fresh eyes. They were leaning towards each other, and their body language said they were a couple. Cynthia's hand was resting on his thigh, suggesting intimacy. So what happened?

She reached for the next envelope and the pages it contained. There was a faint woody smell to the letter. Perhaps it reflected the soap he used, or the aftershave. She unfolded letter and smoothed the creases.

22/12/1958

Cynthia Darling,
*You have no idea how much your response
made my heart sing. I am looking at your*

*painting now, happy that even though I am far
from Pt Reilly, a part of it hangs on my wall. It
is all the more special knowing you painted it. I
feel your presence each time I look at it.*

*Now for my news. I've been thinking about
moving to Pt Reilly permanently. You met my
brother, Robert on our last visit and he loves Pt
Reilly as much as I do. Well not really as much,
because for me Pt Reilly also means you. I have
often spoken to Robert about branching out and
establishing our own business. We would work
well together. I suggested we establish a
practice in Pt Reilly and he agreed! Rents would
be cheap and there is no competition in the
town.*

*My love, this means we can start to plan our
lives together. I'll call you before the end of the
week to let you know when I will be down next.*
Love Gerald

So Gerald was moving to Pt Reilly. What business
would it have been? Jacinta pondered the issue as she
folded the paper and returned it to the envelope. She
glanced at her watch. There wasn't time to keep sitting
here. She needed to so some more sorting and then some
shopping. She retreated to the lounge room to sift through
books and vinyl records, packing them into cardboard
cartons.

With the boxes packed and taped, she transferred her
thoughts to dinner. The supermarket was down the road

and she headed there next, picking up supplies which would allow her to do a fettucine and salmon dish, with a Greek salad, and cheese and fruit to follow. It would be quick and simple.

With another carton packed and the meal organized, Jacinta retreated to the box in the bedroom. She had time to read the last letter before Paul arrived. She pulled it from the bundle.

5/01/1959

Darling Cynthia,

I'm so pleased you like the earrings. As soon as I saw them, I thought of you. Special as they are, they are not the only item of jewelry I have in mind. Robert and I are driving down on Wednesday to complete negotiations for the lease of the new office. We have to come down and back in the one day, but can you meet me for lunch? I feel it so strongly—this is a positive sign for the rest of our lives.

I can't wait until I see you on Wednesday.
All my love,
Gerald

So that's where the tigers eye earrings came from. Jacinta opened the box again, examining them carefully. Symbols of love and adoration. On impulse, she clipped them on her ears. She'd never heard of an engagement, so something must have happened. Why did the letters stop?

By the time Paul arrived, wine in hand, Jacinta had tidied the dining room and set the table with Cynthia's best crockery and cutlery, along with some crystal glasses. She thought Cynthia would approve.

"I hope I'm not late? Something smells good." He proffered the bottle of wine. "Shall I open this?"

"Yes please. I'm more than ready for a drink. I've a feeling the clean-up will take longer than I thought. I keep getting side-tracked by memories. I enjoyed staying here as a child."

"Perhaps you should stay longer," he said. "There's no rush to sell the house, is there? Nice earrings, by the way."

Paul poured the wine and they clinked glasses. "You haven't started on this room yet." He looked around at the paintings on the wall. "This is where I usually sat with Cynthia. I always liked her paintings. My father had one as well."

They stood, admiring the artworks. "Did he?" Jacinta asked. "Cynthia must have given it to him. I don't think she ever sold her work."

"She didn't give it to him. She gave it to dad's brother, Gerald. Dad ended up with it after the accident."

A band of dread tightened around her chest. "What accident? What happened?"

Paul swirled his wine around his glass, studying it before he took a sip. "They were driving down to Pt Reilly from the city. This was when they were planning to move here and had a meeting to finalize a lease on premises they wanted to rent. There was an accident. A drunk driver cleaned them up. Gerald didn't survive."

Tears sprang to Jacinta's eyes. Cynthia must have been devastated. No wonder she'd never married.

Paul reached out and placed his hand over hers. "Now I've upset you. It was a long time ago. I don't think anyone remembers it now. Dad still established his practice here, but it was as a sole practitioner, not in a partnership. Not until I graduated and moved back to Pt Reilly."

Jacinta blinked, clearing her eyes. "I'm okay." *I was just sad for an opportunity and a love that was lost.* She gave a reassuring smile. "Take a seat, and I'll dish up our meal."

Paul reached for the bottle of wine and topped up their glasses. "Did you know there's a cinema in town? There are some good movies on at the moment." He looked up from the task, his eyes seeking hers. "Have you ever thought about moving to Pt Reilly?"

This story was short-listed for the 2019 Little Gems Short Story Award conducted by Romance Writers of Australia, and was first published in the 2019 Little Gems Anthology. The characters here appear later in the Sandy Bay series.

To learn more of this community, you can download the free novella in the series, <u>Secrets in Sandy Bay</u> or type <u>books2read.com/Secrets-at-Sandy-Bay</u> into your browser.

Emily Hussey

Change of Heart

TAYLA ADJUSTED HER headset and peered into the darkness
ahead as the aircraft descended towards the Kings Creek
Airstrip. The cloudy and moonless night didn't help
visibility. On cue, beams of light appeared adjacent to the
strip. Station vehicles with their headlights on were
positioned opposite the touchdown point, and then further
down adjacent to the windsock.

She glanced at Jack, noting the look of intense
concentration as he adjusted the power and lowered a stage
of flaps in preparation for landing.

"Okay, Doc… seatbelts secure, loose articles stashed,
prepare for landing." He cut the power further, easing back
on the stick as they crossed the threshold of the unsealed
strip. The wheels touched with a soft whump about one
hundred meters from the end. As they taxied towards the
parking area adjacent to the sock, they saw a cluster of
people watching their approach. Jack pulled up and cut the
power.

Tayla waited until the propellers stopped windmilling
before she stepped into the cabin behind the cockpit and
opened the side door. Marion, the flight nurse, followed her

out. George Hamilton, the station owner, stepped forward to greet them.

"G'day, Doc. Just a broken leg for you today. Silly bugga got in the way of a bull camel when we were loading the truck. Got a nasty kick. He's in the back of the ute."

"Ouch. That would have hurt." Tayla hurried to where she could see the patient, sitting up on a foam mattress and leaning against the back of the cabin. His pale, pinched expression indicated the degree of pain he must be in, but he still gave her a welcome nod and attempted to smile. The arresting green eyes, contrasting with the tan of his skin, also reflected his pain.

"You were unlucky," Tayla said as she clambered onto the tray of the vehicle. I've treated a few camel bites, but this is the first broken leg."

"Glad to see you, Doc. The things some people will do to get attention," he muttered through clenched teeth. "My own fault. I could see he was getting aggro. I should've kept my distance."

"You'll know better next time. We'll give you something for the pain, put on a splint, and get you back to Alice." Tayla examined the site of the injury, causing the patient to wince and grimace. "Sorry, I'll be as gentle as I can. George's diagnosis is correct. It's broken."

While she had been talking, Marion and Jack had unloaded the stretcher from the rear of the aircraft. "I'll give you something for the pain, then we'll splint your leg. That will keep the fracture stable for the flight back to Alice."

She, Marion, and Jack were a well-rehearsed team. Within minutes, they had a splint secured around the injured leg and had manoevred the patient onto the gurney. Moving it over the uneven surface of the ground was a challenge, but George applied some additional muscle to the task as they wheeled him to the plane and then loaded him on. The Flying Doctor aircraft could accommodate passengers on stretchers, and had all the equipment one would expect in an air ambulance.

Marion took down the patient's history and personal details, and then the door was slammed shut. They strapped themselves in, and with the assistance again of the vehicles lighting up the strip with their headlights, Jack applied power and the aircraft took off, climbing over the homestead and turning on a heading for Alice Springs.

*****

The flight back to Alice was uneventful. Tayla joined Marion sitting in the cabin instead of alongside Jack up front. Marion engaged him in conversation to take his mind off the pain, and they learned that his name was Scully, and he'd been in Australia for six months. His cousin, who was a station hand on Kings Creek station, had found him a job helping with the camel round up. The beasts were headed to the Arabian market.

"I heard about snakes, spiders, and sharks before coming to Oz, but nobody warned me about the camels. I thought this was a great opportunity to see a side of the country that tourists don't often get to see."

"You weren't wrong about that," Tayla said with a wry smile. "Life out here is quite different to what you will find on the Gold Coast or those other locations that tourists usually flock to. What do you do when you're not wrangling camels? Herding cats?"

He didn't quite manage a laugh, but attempted a smile. The pain relief hadn't completely dulled the agony. "I had a small boutique brewery back in Ireland, and got bought out by a larger company. I had no idea what next, so when Connor suggested I join him out here, I jumped at the chance. I thought it would be a change from herding drunken Irishmen. Now, I'm not so sure."

Jack called over his shoulder that they were about to commence their descent. The lights of the town could be seen in the distance, and Tayla knew that a road ambulance would be awaiting their arrival at the airport. She and Marion tightened their seatbelts again, and prepared for landing.

Tayla supervised his loading into the vehicle. She was driving her own car back to town, but Marion would ride with him in the ambulance. The hospital staff would take over his care.

Still on his stretcher, Scully waved her off with a wink. "Thanks for coming, Doc. It was grand meeting you. Wish it was under different circumstances."

It impressed Tayla that the man could attempt to flirt, even when in acute pain. Flirtatious patients came with the job, and she had long since learned to put them in their place. Cute accent though. She was always a sucker for a soft Irish brogue. Come to think of it, he was cute too.

***

The following morning, Tayla checked which ward Scully was in and dropped in for an update on his condition. His leg had been x-rayed, and with an IV drip delivering pain relief, he seemed to be more comfortable, although a little sleepy. She checked the flow of the drip and then picked up his chart hanging at the end of the bed. Scully stirred at her movement, with his eyes flickering open briefly before closing again.

"Morning, Doc," he muttered with his eyes still closed. "I hope you slept better than I did."

"Sorry to hear that. I see from your chart that it was a clean break. You're lucky it was the tibia and not the femur. Let the nursing staff know if you need more pain relief. That will help you to get a good night's sleep."

"I thought the camel had followed me in here," he protested. "Someone was bellowing in the middle of the night."

Tayla laughed sympathetically. "Hospitals can be a bit noisy at night, depending on the ward. You should be able to leave by tomorrow. Do you have somewhere to stay?"

"That's problem number two. I need to find somewhere local while I have follow-up treatment. I've been told I'll need physiotherapy as well."

"You will. What's problem number one? Do you need someone notified of where you are?"

He shook his head. "Only my mam, and I told Connor not to worry her. I'll tell her myself once I'm mobile again.

I left a bag back at the station, and I'm worried it might not be there by the time I get back."

Tayla glanced around the room and saw a duffle bag in the corner. "We loaded a bag in the aircraft with you last night."

He followed the direction of her gaze. "That holds a change of clothes and a bit of dirty washing. This was a small bag tucked away in the chest of drawers in my room. I was staying in the stockman's quarters, so it's not terribly secure."

"Can someone put it aside for you?"

He pressed the button to raise the head end of the bed and elevating him into a sitting position. "They'll have to. Before I came to the Territory, I stopped off in the sapphire fields in Queensland. I've always wanted to try my hand at fossicking. I intended visiting the opal fields next and even noodling for gold. You can do it all in this country."

"Sure, though not many people do. So, you have a bag full of sapphires, opals and gold? No wonder you're worried about it."

"Just some sapphires. I got lucky. They're in the raw state, but should come up a treat when they're cut and polished."

An orderly pushing a wheelchair appeared in the doorway. "Scully O'Riordan? I'm taking you to get your splint put on."

The orderly pushed the chair close to the bed, and Scully slid sideways and onto the seat, desperately trying to hold the edges of his hospital gown together at the back. Not before Tayla caught sight of a pair of tight buns. She grinned to herself at his embarrassment. Nothing she hadn't seen many times before.

***

Did she have to be standing behind him when he slid out of bed, flashing his arse to all and sundry? He hadn't paid a lot of attention to the doctor during the flight into town, but now that he had seen her in the light of day, Scully was impressed. He hadn't expected that the flying doctor would be a woman, let alone someone relatively young and definitely attractive. His time in Australia was full of surprises. If the orderly hadn't turned up when he did, it might have been possible to find out more about her, but then, weren't there issues with doctor-patient relationships? Scully boyo, you'll have to get better right fast.

***

Gemma had a busy day. A car accident on the road to Harts Range required a medical evacuation, and a newborn at Branson Springs decided to make an early arrival. She didn't deliver many babies, and was relieved when mother and baby were healthy following their ordeal. The mother had been preparing to drive to town in anticipation of the impending birth, but the baby decided to take matters into his own hands. He spent the flight in the humidicrib in the aircraft, but looked to be healthy, though tiny.

Tayla dropped into the Hotel Alice that evening, and debriefed the day with a few friends. They were all either medical or aviation people, and understood the pressures of her daily routine.

"Delivered a baby today?" Mark asked. "That's special. Is the mother going to name the baby after you?"

"He's a boy, so I suspect not." Mark was a chopper pilot, who worked on contract, with a mixture of aerial mustering and photographic work. "It's never a dull moment around here. Yesterday, we picked up an Irishman who'd been kicked by a camel."

"That will be a story for him to take back home."

"His leg was broken, so he'll be stuck here for a while. He's looking for accommodation for few weeks after he's discharged. Don't you have a spare room, now that Chris has moved out?"

"Yes, but—"

"It will be good for you to have company. I'll tell him early tomorrow. He should be discharged shortly after that."

Mark sighed dramatically. "Has anyone every told you you're a bully? I'm not sure I need a leprechaun in my spare room."

Tayla thought of the man lying in the hospital bed. He would never be six feet tall, but leprechaun he was not. His dark curly hair combined with curious green eyes indicated that perhaps an ancestor landed on Irish shores with the Spanish Armada. His charisma shone through, even when he was in pain. Helping out a traveller in need was the right thing to do. The opportunity of connecting with him again after discharge had nothing to do with it.

She smirked. "Who me… a bully? A female doctor in this town needs to be assertive, that's all. I learned that in my first week on the job. Besides, you'll get lonely living on your own."

"I'll think about it, okay? I'm fussy about who I live with."

Tayla smiled and bought him another drink.

***

Scully, with a pair of crutches supporting his forearms, was discharged the following morning. Tayla had wrangled the spare key from Mark and had given Scully the address.

"I'd drop you off if I could, but I'm on duty so you'll have to take a taxi. Mark will be home late afternoon. In the meantime, make yourself comfortable. He said to make yourself a tea or coffee. He can take you to the supermarket later so you can do some shopping."

"Thank you. Your friend has been very kind to a stranger. I'll probably just rest this afternoon. I still need to catch up with some sleep, and the pain killers make me a bit dopey. I'll be right as rain by tomorrow though," he added confidently.

One of the hospital volunteers carried his bag downstairs to the taxi rank, detouring past the cafeteria on the way so that he could buy a sandwich for his lunch. It felt strange to be staying with someone he hadn't even met, but as he'd discovered, the Territory was a welcoming place. As long as you didn't abuse the hospitality, you were always welcome.

Mark lived in a large bungalow that had been subdivided into three flats. Everyone who lived in the complex was involved in aviation in one form or another. Scully found the key under the mat as instructed, and made himself comfortable in the room that was obviously the spare room. He crawled onto the bed with relief and closed his eyes. Just that brief morning's activity had exhausted him.

He awoke on hearing the front door open. Footsteps crossed the floor of the living room before a tousled head poked around his bedroom door.

"You obviously found your way here. Sorry I wasn't here when you arrived. I'm Mark."

Scully pushed himself into a sitting position. He swung his feet over the side of the bed, and extended his hand. "Scully. No need to apologise. I'm grateful for the bed. I'm not sure where I would have stayed otherwise. If the Doc hadn't suggested this, I would have been camped in the riverbed."

He grabbed his crutches from where they had been leaning against the wall, and manoevred his way into the living room, dropping gratefully onto a kitchen chair.

Mark kicked off his shoes and dumped his backpack on the floor. "The Doc, as you call her, can be quite persuasive. She's a good doctor though and we love her."

Scully took note of the last comment. He had no idea of the Doc's relationship status, but perhaps she and Mark had something going on. That could be why he agreed to an unexpected guest. "I'll pay you board of course. I'm not sure how long I'll have to stay, but I'm not a free-loader."

A knock sounded at the door a second before it swung open. "I thought I'd drop in on my way home and check if Scully was settled and coping. How's the pain?"

"You're doing house calls now?" Mark's raised eyebrows indicated his bemusement. "Next time I have a headache, you can come and mop my fevered brow."

"In your dreams. This is just a social call." She looked towards Scully, waiting for his answer.

"I slept most of the afternoon. I left hospital with a supply of pain killers, but I don't want to rely on them. I'll be more mobile by tomorrow."

"I picked up some snags and bits and pieces on the way home," Mark said, "and thought I could fire up the barbie, if that's okay with you two?"

"I didn't come here for dinner," Tayla protested.

Scully instantly felt a little better. *Yeah, but I hope you stay.* "If it's not too much trouble... that would be great. I'll cook for you another day, but probably an Irish stew." He was secretly relieved to not have to worry about food this evening, and the Doc staying as well was a bonus.

"Thanks for organising this, Doc. I don't think I thanked you properly before."

"Tayla. The name's Tayla. You're not in hospital any more so you can be less formal." She turned to Mark. "Do you have any salad vegetables in your fridge? I'll throw a salad together while you fire up the grill. No, you stay where you are," she said to Scully as he attempted to rise. "We've got this under control."

Scully felt useless as the other two busied themselves with the makings of dinner. In spite of Tayla's instruction, he followed Mark outside to watch as the other man lit the grill and laid the sausages and chicken shasliks on top.

"Come to watch a master chef?" Mark waved the tongs theatrically. "This is a dry argument though. Can I get you a drink? I've got a beer in the fridge."

"Thanks, but I'll stick with something cold and soft for now. I don't want to mix alcohol with pain killers."

"Smart man. Keep your eye on the snags while I fetch the drinks."

Scully plopped down at the outside table and sniffed appreciatively. There was something about the smell of a barbecue that whetted the appetite. It was a vast improvement on hospital food.

"Get that into you." Mark shoved a cold can of Lemon Solo in his direction. "What's happening with your job? Are you planning on heading back to Kings Creek when you're back on your feet?"

"By that time, the camel mustering will be over, so I am not sure if there will be anything for me to do. I need to get back at some stage though, as I left a small bag behind in my accommodation. I need to pick it up."

"I might be able to help. I'll be down that way in a couple of days. I've got an aerial photography job over Kings Canyon. If you let George know I'm coming, I can drop in and pick it up for you."

The idea of just 'dropping in' at a station that was a couple of hundred kilometres away was impressive. Maybe he should be a helicopter pilot in his next life. "That would be fantastic. I'll let George know. I need to give him an update on my progress anyway."

A shadow fell over them both. Scully looked around to see Tayla silhouetted in the doorway, blocking the light that streamed out from the room behind her. The contrast between light and shadow accentuated the curves and contours of her body, highlighting her femininity in a subtle yet enticing manner. As a doctor, she was all efficiency and business, but in this environment, she was an intriguing and captivating woman.

She paused in the doorway for a fraction of a second before joining them and placing a salad bowl on the table.

"I'll grab the plates and some cutlery." She hurried back inside.

"Tayla obviously knows her way around your kitchen," Scully said to Mark, hoping for an indication on the status of their relationship.

"She's here often enough," Mark said prodding at the sausages. "There's a good crowd with the local aviation community, and the Flying Doctor is part of that. They're often around here for a barbecue or a debrief over a beer or a gin and tonic. She's smart enough to live somewhere nice and quiet. All the rowdy stuff takes place here."

That didn't tell him everything, but gave him some information. For a start, he knew she would be a regular visitor, but he still had questions about her relationship with Mark.

"These are about done," Mark announced, loading a platter with the grilled meat. Tayla had brought out everything else they needed. They ate outside, with the cool night air a refreshing change from the heat of the day. An evening breeze played around the table, and the sounds of night birds and insects occasionally were heard. It was a calming time of day.

"What are your plans while you're here?" Tayla asked.

"I hadn't made any. I bypassed Alice when I travelled to Kings Creek station so I haven't seen anything of the town or it's surrounds. I'd like to do some exploring though, as much as I'm able."

"I'm rostered off on Sunday. I could take you out to Jessie and Emily Gaps if you're up for a drive. You wouldn't have to walk too far. The Gaps are breaks in the MacDonnell Ranges, and have significance to the first nation's people in this area."

She made no mention of Mark coming with them. That had to be a good sign. "I'd like that."

"Great. I'll pick you up here early afternoon. Wear a hat."

***

Tayla looked forward to the afternoon's excursion. She deliberated over the clothes to wear while getting ready. If she was catching up with the usual crew, she would just pull on a pair of khaki shorts and a cotton top—something cool and no fuss. This was different. She still wanted to look casual, as though she hadn't made a special effort, but not like a total slob either. She settled on navy cotton three-quarter length pants, topped with a loose tunic top with a white background covered in shades of blue, over-blown florals. She grabbed a white straw hat, as the Centralian sun could be unforgiving. With a smear of sunscreen over her arms and face, she was ready.

Scully looked up with a smile when she knocked on the door and then opened it, without waiting to be invited in. He slung his backpack over his shoulders and picked up the crutches.

"I'm so looking forward to getting out. I managed to walk down the main street yesterday, and visited one of the local galleries, but I'm sure there's a lot more to Alice Springs than shops and tourist outlets."

She led him out to her Subaru SUV. "There is a lot more, but we'll just do the Gaps today. Another day I can take you out to the Telegraph Station, or further afield."

During the drive, she updated him on her week, and some of the call-outs she'd had, without disclosing any identifying or personal details. She explained how John Flynn had started the Flying Doctor Service in the decade following World War One, and as Scully had experienced for himself, it made a huge difference to people needing medical assistance in remote areas of the outback.

They drove through Heavitree Gap, and then crossed the causeway over the bed of the Todd River, and followed the Ross Highway along the side of the MacDonnell Ranges. Emily Gap was the first stop. Tayla parked in the shade of a tree, and explained as much as she knew of the indigenous beliefs associated with the Gaps. They wandered along the paths and admired the rock art still visible decades after it would have been painted. Insects buzzed across the surface of the water hole. The temperature was noticeably cooler between the towering cliff faces, and it was easy to imagine the refuge that would have been provided in years past.

Scully negotiated the uneven surface with his crutches, but seemed relieved to be sitting again when they returned to the car.

"Are you okay?" Tayla asked. "We don't have to go to Jessie Gap if you're finding it tiring on the crutches."

"I'm fine. Now that we've come this far, I don't want to miss the next one. Besides, I can have a short rest as we drive between the two."

Tayla secretly respected the fact that he didn't cave in too easily, but kept an eye on him in case he appeared to be in discomfort. They were the only visitors at Jessie Gap. She parked in the shade again, and close to the path that led between the trees and then the break in the Ranges. They took their time, pausing in places to examine the rock formations or different plants. Scully had a curious nature, and tested her knowledge about the local environment.

They wandered along the path that wound between the cliffs and vegetation that dotted the landscape. Tayla became aware that something small and hard had found its way inside her shoe.

"Do you mind if we stop for a minute? I need to take my shoe off and shake something out." She plopped down on a large rock, and bent down to ease the shoe from her heel.

"Don't move!"

She looked up in astonishment to see Scully with a crutch raised, staring fixedly to one side of the rock. With a sudden movement, he darted forward and hooked the point of the crutch under a snake and flung it away from them.

Tayla jumped up. "What the…?"

"I thought it was a stick or something first of all, but then it started moving around the side of the rock towards you."

"Oo… looks like a King Brown. Nasty, or it would be if it bit." She laid a hand on his arm. "You know they don't randomly attack, right? Best response is just to get out of their way."

He stared in the direction of the snake with a look of horror. "We don't have snakes in Ireland. That's the first one I've seen outside of a zoo."

Tayla still had her shoe in her hand. She shook out the offending pebble and slipped it back on, keeping her eye on the direction the snake had gone. "They can move quite fast, and that one is likely to be pissed-off after it's unexpected flight. Best if we head back towards the car. We'll watch out for any others along the way."

Scully didn't need telling twice, but appeared rather vigilant as they followed the path back to the car.

Rather than take him back to Mark's flat, Tayla drove to a café in town where they could some afternoon refreshments.

"Do they serve whiskey?" Scully asked, still shaking his head incredulously at his close encounter.

"They probably do. You look like you need a double."

"I was only joking, but that serpent wasn't what I was expecting to see today. I'd heard stories about snakes and how venomous they are, but you Aussies spout as much blarney as Paddy. I'm never sure what to believe."

"That's one snake you should definitely avoid." She reached across the table to grasp his hand. "I haven't thanked you properly. Your quick action may have averted a disaster." His hand felt warm in hers.

"Well, I couldn't have driven us back with my leg in a cast," he joked. "I was thinking of myself."

"Really?"

"No… not really. I reacted without thinking. I would have been devastated if any harm had come to you."

Those green eyes looked at her with an intensity that sent a flush from her head to her central core. She drew a quick breath and looked away briefly, lest he see the effect he had on her. Perhaps he had a little Leprechaun magic after all.

"Shall we order?" she asked, changing the subject and regaining her equilibrium. "I can recommend the Vanilla Slice, or failing that, the Chocolate Mud Cake is also good."

"Actually, I might try their craft beer and a plate of tapas with that. This isn't a busman's holiday, but I'm always curious if the local ale is as good as I made back home. This is my shout."

"Sure, if that's what you'd like. Are you going to show the locals how to do it better? This is definitely a town that enjoys a beer."

"You know, that's not a bad idea. When I sold out in Ireland, the contract restricted me from starting a competitive business, but that restriction didn't stretch as far as Alice Springs. You've given me something to think about."

Tayla felt an unexpected surge of happiness. Maybe her Leprechaun with the broken leg would stay longer than the time it took for him to heal. Perhaps it was his lilting accent, or perhaps it was those mischievous eyes. Perhaps it was the way he looked at her, but she, Dr Tayla Nicholson hoped that this man would stick around.

***

The day had been more tiring than he expected, but it was a good sort of tired. He would sleep well the coming night, and hopefully without the need for the painkillers that had helped him through the previous nights.

Scully opened the bag that Mark had brought back from Kings Creek, and removed the pouch from inside. Loosening the drawstring, he tipped out the contents on the bedside table, and pushed the rough stones around with his finger, trying with the eye of a novice to assess each for colour and quality. Finding them had been beginner's luck, or was it the luck of the Irish? He picked up one and held it up to the light to examine it more closely. This particular stone was one he'd been told was most likely to provide a sapphire of high quality when cut.

"Fit to grace the ring on a princess' hand," the old miner had joked.

Scully had laughed at the time, but maybe the old man had been prophetic. He hadn't left Ireland with a particular goal in mind, but when Connor had suggested Australia as a land of surprising opportunity, he'd thought that was as good a reason to visit as any. There was nobody pining for him back on the Emerald Isle, but he had intended to return. Anyone could have a change of heart.

He looked at the special stone once more before carefully returning them all to the pouch. Princesses could be found anywhere as well.

***

Change of Heart is an introductory story for the Red Centre Series (see the description on the following pages). To learn more about the series, download the free novella, Journey to the Heart <u>here</u> or type books2read.com/Journey-to-the-Heart into your web browser.

Wild Card

1

GEMMA RESTED HER head in her hands, massaging her scalp. The level of focus required for the readings drained her. She heard arguing voices outside her tent.

"…but it could be interesting, Saxon. Who knows what I might learn? I just want to—"

"Don't waste your money. If you want tales of tall, dark, handsome strangers, I can give you those and it won't cost a cent."

Another sceptic. Why was he at the CovenFest anyway? The voices trailed off into the distance, but not before Gemma felt the strangest of sensations. A vibration in the air appeared to hum, although there wasn't a sound. She sensed it. The air shimmered in front of her eyes. As she pondered the weird visual effects, they dissipated and the air cleared again.

She had pulled open the curtain over the door of the tent when the last client left, and now a woman peered in with a hopeful expression. "Are you free?"

"Sure. Take a seat and give me something of yours to hold. Don't worry, you'll get it back."

The woman sat, sliding a ring off her finger as she did. She passed it to Gemma, glancing around curiously at the interior of the tent. The drapes in shades of violet, gave it an intimate feel. The table was covered in a deep purple velvet cloth, and a small crystal ball sat on a stand, supported by three tiny metallic angels. A light hung from the centre of the roof, and the stained-glass shade cast colorful glimmers over the scene below.

Gemma focused on the ring and the vibrations she received from the woman. A small soul hovered behind the woman's shoulder, a young child who had not stayed earthside. Gemma repressed the wave of sadness she felt at this understanding, and pushed the deck of cards towards the woman.

"Shuffle these cards for me. While you do that, I can tell you that your daughter is sorry she had to leave you. She is in a happy place, and explains it wasn't her time. Although she has left you in her physical form, she stays close and always will."

The woman's eyes widened at those words, and she brushed away a tear that formed in the corner of her eye. "Will I ever become a mother?"

"You always *will* be a mother," Gemma said gently. "Nothing will change that, but we'll see what the cards tell us."

She dealt the cards from the top of the pack in the spread she judged best suited to answer the woman's question. The High Priestess card featured, plus the eight of coins and the Page of Swords. There were other cards that confirmed that the woman would indeed bear a child, most likely a son, and that should occur in the next eighteen months.

When the reading finished, Gemma flipped the sign outside the tent from *Busy* to *Free'* and added a few drops of lemon myrtle to the oil burner to renew her emotional energy. As she did, she heard the young woman's voice from earlier that day.

"I don't care what you think. I'm going in. You don't have to join me, in fact it's better you don't."

The tent flap was pulled aside, and a young woman poked her head in. "Hi, I'm Sophie. I'd like a reading."

Gemma invited Sophie to sit and repeated the process of psychometry, holding a bracelet which the young woman slipped from her arm.

"This bracelet didn't originally belong to you. The person who gave it to you says that she is pleased that you've done so well academically, and reminds you to visit your grandma more often."

"Oh, that's my mum. I half expected her to say I should tidy my room. I didn't know she would be here."

"She's never far from you." Gemma paused while Sophie reached for the tissue box. "What questions did you want answered today?"

Sophie explained she was trying to decide between two career options, and also wondered about the attentions of a particular young man. Gemma wasn't surprised about either issue. They reviewed the advice shown in the cards, and discussed their interpretation. Gemma finished the session with some sisterly advice arising from her own intuition and experience.

Sophie smiled in relief. "Thank you... you've been so helpful. Saxon will pay. I'll call him." She stood and pulled aside the tent flap, peering past a cluster of people standing outside. "You can come in now".

The man stooped as he entered the tent, with his broad shoulders obscuring the light that moments before had streamed in from outside. When he straightened, his head brushed the silk fabric lining the roof. He gave Sophie a sardonic look.

"So, you're going to come into a fortune in the next year, and a tall dark stranger will sweep you off your feet. You and this stranger will live happily ever after and have ten children."

"Don't be silly. It wasn't like that at all. My mother was here, and that was so reassuring. Can you pay, please?"

The man visibly rolled his eyes, but reached into the pocket of his jacket for his wallet. The hum that Gemma had heard earlier started again. As she tried to focus on the couple standing before her, the air between them began to shimmer. Perhaps she had a migraine coming on. She reached out a hand to take the proffered cash, and nearly jerked back at the zap she experienced when their hands connected. If he had a similar reaction, he didn't comment, but gave her a puzzled look. His attitude irritated her.

"If you sit down, I'll gift you a reading. You might learn if you have a tall, dark stranger in your future. Incidentally, the same person who came forward for Sophie also has a message for you. She says to stop dicking around and suggests that it's time you got replacement for Rusty."

"Rusty?" Sophie looked puzzled.

Saxon looked stunned. "He was my labrador. I had him when your mother and I were kids. You must have told her."

"How could I? I didn't know anything about your dog. Sit down, Saxon. Listen to your reading."

He sat in the chair recently vacated by Sophie. "I'm not sure how you knew that, but only Maretta would tell me to stop dicking around."

Gemma told him to shuffle the cards and asked if he had any questions. Saxon shook his head.

"In that case, I'll provide a general reading according to what the cards tell me." She spread them on the table in front of them and leaned forward to study the connections.

"Hmm… you've come to Leavenworth because of a business venture. It is an exploratory trip to further discussions with a potential partner." She pointed to the Four of Wands. "You need to be on guard. This person has not been honest with you. He is in negotiations with someone else, and I am not even sure if he owns the property that brought you here. Do your due diligence." She studied the next card. "In two days, this deal will come crashing down. Do not outlay any money."

His eyes narrowed. "How can you know that? Who's been talking to you?"

"Nobody has spoken to me. It's what I do. I read situations and the Goddess speaks through me. I can only tell you what I have learned in these last moments. What you do with that information is up to you."

He stared at her skeptically. She saw his eyes stray down to her decolletage, displayed by the low neckline and tightly-laced corset top giving uplift to her exposed breasts. The opal pendant, gifted by her Australian grandmother, sat neatly between them. Surprising her, a warm rush swept over her body. The vibrations were now very intense, making it difficult for her to focus. His glance was so inappropriate. He was here with another woman. She swept her silk shawl across her chest in protective response.

The penultimate card in the spread was The Lovers, followed by the King of Pentangles. "As you can see, there are new beginnings of a passionate kind. As that is presumably not the new business venture, it is more likely to be on the personal level." She looked up as Sophie laughed delightedly, slapping Saxon playfully on the shoulder.

"I told you… you're the one discovering everlasting love."

The affection between the couple was obvious. That must be the basis for the vibration she felt. Usually, for the women in her family, such vibrations were only felt when connections were made with their life partner, but in this instance, she had obviously picked up connection between the couple in front of her. Perhaps their close proximity was the cause.

Gemma nodded in agreement. "I can feel the power of love in your relationship."

Saxon burst out laughing. "That proves you're a phony. Sophie is my niece, not my lover. Thank you for your time, but I'll rely on my own financial acumen when assessing any business ventures."

Sophie flicked her an apologetic look before tugging at her uncle's sleeve. "Time to go if you want some afternoon tea."

His eyes flickered, but he obediently turned and held the tent flap open for his niece to precede him. Only after he had stepped through the gap did he speak again. "I don't know how you know that information, but if I learn that there has been a leak in this deal, I'll be back to speak to you again."

Gemma heaved a sigh of relief when they were gone. The humming stopped and the air cleared. So did her headache. The consultation left her confused. She hadn't experienced those vibrations before. She heard muffled voices outside and mentally prepared herself for a new client.

"Am I interrupting anything?"

Gemma looked up to see a woman peering through the tent flap, grinning widely. It looked like… surely it wasn't… "Cassie!" She sprang out of her chair and the two women embraced. "You didn't tell me you were coming today!"

"Are you finished for the day? What time should we come back? We've checked into the Leavenworth Inn, but I'd love to have dinner with you tonight. We've so much catching up to do."

"Of course, I'm free. It's not every day I get a visit from my cousin in Australia." Gemma glanced at her watch. "Only fifteen minutes to go before official close. It won't take me long to pack up. I'll meet you in the Witches Brew Bar in half an hour. The food's good and we should be able to get a table. Cassie, it's so good to see you. I need to debrief after today."

One more client slipped through the tent flap, so thirty-seven minutes passed before she paused in the doorway of the inn, searching the room for her cousin. They were already seated at a table, and as Gemma approached, Cassie jumped up with a squeal of delight.

The two women embraced again, before Cassie broke away and grasping his hand, dragged forward the man who stood behind her.

"Gemma, I'd like you to meet Daniel, my husband. We're on a combined honeymoon and work trip. Daniel has some meetings to attend in the States, and I'm making the most of the opportunity to connect with other Clans here. I'm developing new markets for my tinctures."

Gemma ignored the proffered hand and seizing Daniel by the shoulders, kissed him on the cheek. "Welcome to the family. I assume I have you to blame for my cousin's condition?"

He blushed, and the two women burst into giggles. Cassie rested her hand protectively on her belly.

"Is it so obvious?

"Even it if weren't your swollen belly, you have a glow about you. Congratulations to you both. I'll fetch us a mulled wine while you make yourselves comfortable… a non-alcoholic version for you" she added, looking meaningfully at Cassie.

The vibe from the Covenfest carried over into the Witches Brew. The outside of the building was draped in Halloween decorations, and many of the stall-holders and exhibitors were already there. Greetings were exchanged fueled by the heightened mood of a successful day. As she picked her way back to the table carrying the tray of drinks, she sensed the low-pitched hum again, and felt gentle vibrations running the length of her spine.

Gemma looked around as she placed the drinks on the table, and caught sight of Saxon and Sophie sitting on the other side of the room. She shook her head to clear the noise. *I'm picking up their connection again.*

Cassie placed a hand on her arm. "Long day? You're looked a bit flustered."

"I'm fine, and all the better for seeing you both. I thought I was getting a migraine earlier, but the symptoms aren't typical. I keep hearing a low hum and the air around me pulses with subtle vibrations."

Cassie's eyes widened. "That's not so strange for the women in our matrilineal line. You know what it means, don't you?"

"Yes, but I'm sure it's not relevant now. Perhaps it only works in Australia. I first felt the vibrations when a couple came to my tent for a reading today. They're also here now, so I must be picking up the vibrations between them. They're related and appear to be very close."

Cassie frowned. "It doesn't usually work like that" She glanced at Daniel with a grin. "It was so strong between us when we first met. I was confused at first, but that's when I had an inkling that I'd found the one."

Daniel laughed. "Helped by a certain concoction this woman distilled. Her tinctures are incredibly powerful."

Gemma knew that her cousin distilled a range of herbal tinctures which had therapeutic uses.

"That reminds me." Cassie pulled a small box from her bag and laid it on the table. She opened the box to reveal three small vials. "These are for you. Only ever ingest a couple of drops at a time. This one is for depression; this treats period pain; and this one…" a smile tugged at her lips as she held up the tiny bottle. "…this one is a powerful aphrodisiac. Use it sparingly and only after careful deliberation."

Daniel nodded. "Cassie had me at *hello*, but I can confirm that a couple of drops of that solution in my wine had an astounding effect."

"There's no-one on my horizon, so the stopper is likely to stay where it is."

Cassie resisted the temptation to open the bottle and sniff. Instead, she slipped the box into her bag, and the two cousins spent the rest of the evening catching up on news, both of family members who still ivied in Cassie's home town of Harrow, and others who now lived in Leavenworth after Gemma's grandmother, Lydia, followed a man she had met and settled down in that community.

She made arrangements to show them around the following day, and introduce them to the attractions of Leavenworth. They only had a short time to spend in the town, but Gemma promised to show them the highlights. When Cassie and Daniel left two days later, it was with a promise extracted from Gemma that she would return the favor and visit them one day in Harrow.

2

GEMMA FELT FLAT after they left. She had enjoyed
showing the visitors around the town and surrounding
country, but their closeness and obvious happiness
reminded her of her single state. She nearly opened the first
of the tincture bottles, before she remembered that this was
also a time of changing seasons, and typically this was also
a time when emotions were likely to be at their lowest.

She needed to undertake a cleansing ritual to prepare
herself for the winter and the quiet times ahead. Winter was
a time of regrouping and reflection… how many times had
she explained this to those who came to her for advice? She
needed to heed her own words. The sun still shone brightly
each day, but with waning warmth. Soon it would be too
cold for her plans.

Having grown up in Leavenworth, she knew all the
trails along the river and the secret places where she was
unlikely to be disturbed. She undressed, and slipped a long
robe over her naked body. Gathering the things she needed
in a small bag, she drove to the parking area near the river
and made her way along the edge of the river bank until she
reached an area she knew to be secluded. Not many people
would be in the area on a weekday. The grotto, surrounded
by spruce trees, was perfect. A carpet of dried leaves lined
the ground.

She lit a smudge stick and cleansed the air around her
and then filled a crystal goblet with red wine. She sipped
slowly before raising the goblet to the skies and then
dashing some of the wine on the ground. "Mother Demeter,

receive my libation in honor of your care and guidance as we transition from the days of autumn towards the time of reflection and regeneration in the winter months. Watch over us in our days of slumber, and when we awaken from the quiet times, guide us towards the times of regeneration."

She placed the goblet on the ground, and then lifted the robe over her head, standing in her naked glory. A few paces took her to the water's edge, and she stepped gingerly into the cold water, wading out towards the middle of the river. The cold that enveloped her midriff caused her to involuntarily gasp. She breathed out slowly to acclimatize herself to the temperature, then taking another breath, submerged herself beneath the surface.

The cool water was invigorating, and when she opened her eyes, she could see the smooth rocks on the bottom, and tiny fish swimming around them. She surfaced and floated for a while, with her long hair streaming behind her. The cold would soon chill her bones, and she knew she needed to leave the water. She pulled herself up on the river bank, grasping at tufts of grass to steady her. Only as she stood with the water streaming down her body did she become aware of the man standing at the edge of the clearing, with a stunned expression on his face.

***

How did that witch of a woman know that his deal was taking a dive? Saxon wanted to clear his head. Best way he knew of doing that was to get out in the fresh air. He drove to the carpark at Waterfront Park, and after locking the car, followed the path along the river bank. Few people were around, given that it was a week day.

Even though Saxon had been skeptical after the warning she'd given him, he'd asked a series of pointed questions in the negotiations. The right answers weren't forthcoming, so he investigated further. There were undisclosed restrictions over the property he was trying to purchase, and which would negatively impact his development. Addressing those issues would cost him as much as the purchase price. He had nearly lost three million dollars, and potentially much more.

The tension that had built up over the last twenty-four hours eased as he followed the trail beside the river. At one point, the path split into two separate options, and after deliberation, he took the smaller of the two. He would meet less people that way, and it took him closer to the water. The over-grown path continued for one hundred yards, and then opened out into a small clearing at the edge of the river.

Items on the ground indicated someone might not be far away. He glanced around, but a slight splashing noise drew his attention back to the water. Saxon stared in astonishment as a naked woman rose from beneath the surface, and waded towards the bank. Water streamed down her body plastering her hair to what he could see of her luscious breasts. All she wore was an opal pendant swinging between those pearly globes. The scene reminded him of the Birth of Venus painted by Botticelli, except this woman wasn't standing on a shell.

Holy crap! I shouldn't be caught alone in the woods with a naked woman. Before he could back away, the woman looked up and their eyes met. She looked just as startled as he felt. She recovered first, and looked at him brazenly, her head on one side and with a hint of laughter in her eyes.

"Since you're standing there, you can pass me my robe, lying on the ground behind you."

She didn't appear the least embarrassed. He picked up the garment, and keeping his face averted, took a few steps towards her and held it out in her direction. It was taken from his hand and he heard the slither of fabric as it was pulled over her head.

"It's okay… you can look now."

When he faced her again, she wore a long gown that clung to her damp body, outlining her figure perfectly. As best he could make out, she looked bemused rather than alarmed. A shimmering in the air between them made him shut his eyes, then blink rapidly to clear his vision.

On opening them again, he noted two things. One; standing before him was the woman who read the cards at the CovenFest; and two, she now looked at him as though she had seen a ghost. Her lips moved, but he struggled to hear what she said. Sounded like *…again… the hum… it can't be…*

"Sorry, I didn't catch that."

"You weren't meant to. I was thinking out loud."

"Do you often skinny dip in the river where anyone could see you?"

"Only when I'm cleansing as part of a ritual, and only where I don't expect an audience. You didn't have to look."

"It wasn't a choice. You rose out of the river in front of me. If you'd had a sign up further back along the track saying 'Private bathing ahead', I would have turned around and gone back."

She tilted her head to one side with eyes half-closed as she considered those words. "No, you wouldn't. A man like you doesn't like to be prevented from doing anything he wants."

Saxon threw back his head and laughed. "Is that in the cards, or is an ethereal visitation advising you of that fact? You're right... I probably would have pushed on. Come to think of it, I'm not sorry that I did. It wasn't a sight I expected, but I feel infinitely better than I did before my walk."

She shrugged. "Put it down to intuition based on an understanding of human behaviour."

"I'm Saxon, by the way."

"I know. I'm Gemma." She wrung some of the water from her hair and picked up a goblet and bottle of wine from the ground. "I won't apologize for disturbing your walk, as you don't appear distressed. I bid you farewell."

With her bag slung over her shoulder, she ducked around him and headed towards the overgrown path.

"Wait! I wanted to thank you, and I'd still like to know how you knew what you did. You've saved me a significant financial loss."

She paused by the entrance to the path. "No need to thank me. I'm pleased for your sake that you heeded my advice."

Saxon knew he couldn't let her simply disappear. She intrigued him, and the fact that he knew she was naked under that robe had nothing to do with it. "I want to thank you properly. Will you have dinner with me tonight?"

An expression he couldn't interpret crossed her face as she regarded him, not speaking for a moment. "Sure. Meet me at the Witches Brew Tavern at seven. See you then." She turned abruptly and pushing aside the bushes at the entrance to the path, disappeared from view.

***

The vibrations… they were so strong! Gemma didn't normally run away from life's challenges, but she needed to remove herself from Saxon's presence while she processed what she had felt. The low-pitched hum grew softer and ceased as she put some distance between them, but the sensation when he had handed her the robe and her hand had brushed against his had been electric. Why had Saxon come into her life, and why now?

She recalled Cassie's comments. The vibrations between her and Daniel had been so strong, and that's the way it had been for her mother before her, and indeed for all the women in the clan. Gemma had assumed that this was an ability that was only experienced in Australia, and since her grandmother had migrated long ago, any such ability to recognize a life-partner would have long since faded. Normally, she didn't date people from outside the community, but the invitation for this evening was something different. That was why she had agreed to have dinner with him.

She arrived early at the tavern, wanting to assess the atmosphere before Saxon arrived, and then to measure the intensity of any vibrations that accompanied him. She chose a secluded booth away from the general activity, where they would be able to talk in private. It also meant she could watch him before he saw her.

A flurry of excitement enveloped her when she saw him pause in the doorway. With her intuitive abilities, she should have known more about him than she did, but it was easier to provide information for people other than herself. Her eyes widened as she realized that he wasn't alone. The presence she had sensed in her tent the day of the Covenfest was behind him again. On the periphery of her vision, she saw a slender hand reach out and push Saxon in her direction.

His eyes lit up when he saw her, and he threaded his way around the evening revelers towards her.

"You're here," he said with a note of surprise in his voice. "I wasn't sure if you would turn up, after our earlier encounter."

"If I had concerns with others seeing me skyclad, I wouldn't have removed my robe in the first place. Not that I expected to encounter anyone," she added. "Is your niece with you?"

"Sophie only came for the weekend. She badgered me about coming to Leavenworth to experience the Covenfest, but she had to catch the train back to Seattle for work. I came here to pursue the negotiations, not because of any witchy-poo events."

Witchy-poo? Did he view her as some sort of sideshow event? He should know better than to annoy a witch. He probably expected her to have a bubbling cauldron at home, boiling up bat wings and eyes of newt, or something like that. Her abilities were far more subtle, but just as effective.

"What would you like to drink? He asked. "I'll order from the bar and then perhaps you can give recommendations on the menu."

"I'll get it. I know you're a scotch and soda man." She clicked her fingers and moments later a water appeared at their table with a scotch and soda for him, and a cider for her.

"How did you do that? Is there some sort of secret communication system here?" He looked from her to the bar and back again, as though he might see a visible link. There was none.

"Just put it down to witchy-poo skills." In fact, she had seen him drinking scotch and soda after the CovenFest, and before he arrived, she had teed up with Sam behind the bar, that when she clicked her fingers, he would bring over the requested drinks and put them on her tab. Saxon looked both amazed and impressed.

"You're a lady of many talents. How did you know the details of the acquisition that brought me to town?"

That was not so easy to explain. "Many of the people who live in this town have non-conventional abilities. I read the cards as you know, but I'm also a medium. The Goddess speaks through me. I learn a lot about my clients as we sit across the table from each other. As a child, I thought everyone did this. As I grew older, I understood that although many people have well-developed intuition, my gift is more extensive. I can tell you now that your sister, Sophie's mother, still hasn't forgiven you for losing her favorite bear."

"That was years ago! We were kids. She can't still hold that against me."

"I think she's teasing you. She's watching out for your interests though, and she knew there was something off about that deal. She communicated that information through me."

Saxon was silent for a while as he digested this information. "We were close growing up, so it's not surprising that she's still watching out for me."

Gemma laid a consoling hand on his arm. This time the response was unmistakable. She felt a distinct jolt and the hum in her ears was momentarily deafening. Saxon didn't comment, but rubbed at his arm as though it was itchy and his grey eyes looked slightly puzzled.

She was keenly aware of the presence of the man sitting opposite. She watched those well-formed lips as he talked about his work, and wanted to reach out and run a finger around their edges. More than that, she wanted to press her lips against his, losing herself in their plump fullness.

His quizzical expression and the sudden silence made her aware that he had asked her a question and waited for a response. She had been lost in thoughts of what she would like to do to him and with him. She felt a heated flush rise over her cheeks.

"It's a little warm in here. Sorry, I was distracted by the music. What did you just say?"

The knowing look he gave her suggested he hadn't been fooled and knew exactly what she had been thinking. That was impossible. She was the one with ISP, not him.

"I said I should leave tomorrow. If this acquisition has fallen through, there's no point in staying longer."

"If it's not confidential, what were you proposing to do with the property you wanted to acquire?"

"Establish a health and lifestyle retreat with a rural feel. It would have provided a range of health and relaxation modalities for either people on their own, or couples or larger groups."

"It's a wonderful idea, but have you explored all the options? Who were you negotiating with?"

"Silas McGregor."

I should have guessed it would be him. Of all people, Saxon had to get involved with the most dangerous man in town.

Her attention was caught by the protracted stare of a man standing at the bar. Her heart sank. Silas McGregor himself. The look was not friendly. When he saw that she had noticed him, he raised one hand and forming the shape of a gun with his fingers, pointed it at her, pretending to shoot. She closed her eyes momentarily, focusing on erecting a force-field around her and Saxon.

"You were well out of that deal, but there may be others. Why don't you chat to the local realtors tomorrow, and see what other properties might be available?

Saxon regarded Gemma with a speculative look. "That's not a bad idea. If you're free, you could come with me. You may have some insights on the options based on your local knowledge and well… your other abilities."

Gemma didn't want to appear too eager, but it would give her a legitimate excuse to spend more time in his company. She fingered her opal pendant, as though giving the matter serious consideration, before smiling and agreeing. "Of course, I will."

Ben, resident singer at the inn, began the first song of the evening, making conversation difficult. They listened to a couple of brackets, then by mutual agreement, called it a night. Saxon was walking back to his hotel, but accompanied Gemma to her vehicle. She paused on reaching it, and turned to face him. He stood with one hand against the side of the car, looking down at her. She hadn't appreciated before how tall he was.

With a table no longer between them, she was acutely aware of his proximity and the body heat he exuded. Full moon was a couple of days prior, but there was still enough light to highlight his face and the eyes that watched her. Surely, he could sense the vibrations in the air between them, or was that just the beating of her heart? Her gaze moved from his eyes to those lips, and as she did, he reached out, sliding a finger down the side of her face before blotting out the light of the moon as he lowered his head to hers and claimed her mouth.

She felt her the walls of her chest tighten, and her knees weaken as she slumped against him, savoring the sensation of those gorgeous lips. The vibration morphed into a musical hum. A night bird swooped low overhead, calling a raucous greeting, or was it a warning? In that moment, she came to her senses. Her body might be screaming for his touch, but her head wasn't ready. She broke away from his grasp, pushing at his chest, and gasping for air.

Saxon released his hold on her. "I'm sorry… I'm not usually so forward. I didn't mean to take advantage of the situation."

He didn't look sorry at all, but Gemma let that pass. Nor was she, but this was a relationship to savor, and groping each other while leaning against her car was not the way to do that. She opened the door and slid inside.

3

SITTING ACROSS THE table from her had been a torment. There was something about Gemma, and it wasn't just that he had already seen her naked. If he was honest, that experience, although unexpected, had awakened a response more powerful that he usually felt with a woman. Hiding that had been a major effort. He felt an attraction for her stronger than he had with anyone else. It made the suggestion of spending another day in Leavenworth more appealing.

He hadn't intended to kiss her, but the opportunity had been compelling. He should practice some self-restraint, no matter how enticing the woman. Until she pushed him away, she gave every indication of being a very willing participant. He was confused just thinking about it.

Saxon picked her up at the address she had given him the night before, surprised at the sudden rush he felt when he saw her approaching his car. He had a feeling this was going to be a day to remember, and he didn't need to be psychic for that.

"I hope you slept well," she said with a side-eye look.

"Absolutely. I had the most amazing dreams. I can only hope they are an omen of what the future brings."

She looked at him with a bemused smile. If her talents ran to reading minds, he was going to be in trouble. His dreams had definitely been X-rated, in the crazy fashion that dreams had. He tried to make his mind a blank, except for focusing on the inspections.

"I've got a couple of properties to inspect, and the realtor will meet us at the first address."

He gave her the slip of paper on which he had written the addresses. She directed him to the location where the realtor already waited. The main house had several bedrooms and spacious reception areas. It also had a small cottage in the grounds, and there was room for extension to create the development he envisaged. The second property was similar, but had more extensive gardens and an indoor swimming pool. There were pros and cons with each property, and Saxon decided he needed time to assess those options.

"There is one more possibility," Gemma said slowly. "Land overlooking the Wenatchee River. There is some for sale. You could build a purpose-designed facility instead of adapting something that is already constructed. I'll show you.

Saxon shrugged in acquiescence. "I'm in your hands."

Gemma directed him over some rural roads to reach it from the location of their last property. It took them through Okanogan-Wenatchee Forest, a route that only locals were likely to know. They weren't travelling particularly fast, given the bends in the road, which was just as well. Suddenly, a deer dashed across the road and front of them and Saxon skidded to a halt but he still heard a soft bump.

"Fuck! It came out of nowhere. Did I hit it?" Saxon opened his door, preparing to get out of the car.

"Don't get out!" Gemma reached out attempting to grab at his arm.

He looked at her in confusion. "But I have to check…" Without waiting for her to reply, he slid out from behind the wheel. The snarl he heard came out of nowhere. Twisting around, he was confronted by a bear—a large black bear standing upright and advancing towards him. The deer was nowhere to be seen. He tried to remember everything he'd heard about bears. Keep still, don't turn your back, they rarely kill… He hoped the bear had read the same advice. By the look of the bared teeth and the unsheathed claws, it hadn't.

The passenger door slammed, and Gemma stood with the car between her and the advancing beast. Was the woman crazy? "Gemma—stay in the car!" She ignored him and grasping the edge of the car roof, began a haunting chant. The air shimmered around her.

"Lady Diana, hear my prayer. I need your strength, courage, and protection. Deliver us from the evil that threatens us now."

The skies darkened, even though it was the middle of the day. A loud clap of thunder caused the car to rock and the bear halted, peering towards the sky. After a moment, it dropped onto all fours and turned and ambled towards the undergrowth in the forest.

"What just happened?" Saxon looked at Gemma in bewilderment, then back to the bear, wanting to be sure it was gone. He didn't see the beast, but he did see the back of a man dodging through the trees.

Gemma instructions were curt. "Get in. It isn't safe here. We've offended the wrong person."

"Like who?"

"Silas McGregor. You're lucky I was with you, but then, he's also aware that I gave you the warning about dealing with him, so he has me in his sights, probably more so than you. Fortunately, I have connections of my own."

Saxon started the car again, this time driving while looking in all directions as well as straight ahead. Gemma laid a reassuring hand on his shoulder.

"We're not all like that. Leavenworth is a popular town, and for good reason. This is a close community, but we're united for the common good. Don't let extremists like Silas scare you off."

He glanced at her quickly, not wanting to take his eyes off the road, but long enough to note the beseeching look in her extraordinary green-amber eyes. "Lucky I don't scare easily."

When they reached the location she had in mind, Saxon climbed from the car and stood in awe. The site overlooked the river with a magnificent view. "This was an inspired suggestion. It's better than anything we looked at earlier."

"We aim to please," Gemma said coquettishly.

In a spontaneous gesture, he reached out and grasped her around her shoulders. "I owe you so much. I don't know how I'll repay you, but let me start by joining me for dinner this evening."

"Why don't you let me cook *you* dinner? If you're going to be involved with the town, you need to see more than the inside of a motel."

"I can do a reading for you as well."

"You've won me on both counts."

***

The time spent in his company had convinced Gemma that his destiny and hers were closely entwined, but did he understand that? She couldn't let him just disappear and assign any negotiations to an assistant. She had a couple of hours after he dropped her back home in which to shop for ingredients and to prepare the meal. Simplicity was best. She settled on Lemon Chicken with a green salad and rosemary potatoes, followed by a mixed berry and white chocolate mousse for dessert. The final ingredient she wanted sat on the kitchen bench. The urge to open the stopper and smell the contents was strong, but heeding Cassie's warning, she resisted. She wouldn't use it until just before serving. The sweet berries would disguise any flavor.

By the time the doorbell rang, the table was set and the meal ready to be served. Two bowls of prepared dessert sat under a cover in the kitchen.

"I couldn't come empty-handed." Saxon held out a bottle of sparkling wine, and a bunch of roses." He kissed her cheek as he handed over the flowers. "You look stunning,"

Saxon was dressed casually in an open-necked shirt and a pair of jeans. Gemma smiled as she ran a finger down the exposed area of his chest, finishing at the top button. "Flattery will get you everywhere. You're looking rather hot yourself. You open the wine while I find a vase for the flowers."

He complied with the self-assurance of a man who was comfortable in her company. She wasn't sure if the way to a man's heart was through his stomach, but he made appreciative comments all through the meal, in between telling her of his plans in greater detail and taking aboard some of her suggestions as well.

He patted his stomach with satisfaction. "Congratulations to the cook. I couldn't eat another thing."

"Surely you could handle dessert? It's something light."

Not waiting for his response, she slipped back to the kitchen. After opening the tiny bottle, she added a drop to each bowl, then carried them back to the dining table. His eyes widened, but Saxon picked up his spoon and tasted the berries.

"So sweet! They have a really delicate flavor. I don't think I can resist."

After watching while he ate the first spoonful, Gemma tasted her own berries. Saxon was right. They tasted delicious.

The whole evening, she had been conscious of the connection between them. The vibrations were not as strong as when they had first met, and had now settled to a comfortable background hum. Now, she noticed a soft violet aura at the periphery of her vision, and the strangest sensations teased her body. She could almost swear that she had engaged in acts of delicious sensory stimulation, but Saxon hadn't touched her.

Her breath caught in her throat as she looked at him, and her breasts swelled in response. They tingled and screamed to be touched, with her pebbled nipples straining against the constraints of her clothing. She grabbed at her wine and sipped, absorbing the feelings sweeping over her body as the tiny bubbles exploded in her mouth.

"Have I told you what an incredible woman you are?" Saxon husked, looking dazed and slightly flushed as though feeling the heat. He undid a couple of buttons on his shirt. "I'm feeling a little warm. Must be the wine."

"I'll fetch you some water." Perhaps she had made a dreadful mistake. She had no idea how potent the tincture was. Gemma filled a glass in the kitchen, but when she turned to carry it back to the table, Saxon stood behind her.

"I didn't want to make you run around after me. You've done so much already."

She looked up at him, noticing that his eyes, previously an intriguing grey, now appeared to be dark pools in which she could drown. He took the glass from her and took a gulp before placing it on the counter behind her.

"You witch of a woman… no-one has ever made me feel like this before. Stop me if I'm out of line, but I have an irresistible urge to kiss you."

Stop you? Why would I do that? This time, she wouldn't push him away. Gemma raised her lips to his, sliding her arms around his body and softly massaging the area of his back beneath his fingers. "Shut up and kiss me," she whispered before he claimed her mouth with a hunger that spoke of yet a greater desire. Tentatively, his tongue touched hers, tasting of sweet berries. They broke off to draw breath, and his eyes now asked a wordless question.

"I'll help you cool off," Gemma murmured, wrenching the shirt from inside his jeans and undoing the remainder of his buttons. She slid her hands over his muscled torso, never losing eye contact.

"Aren't you feeling the heat as well? Saxon asked huskily.

"It is a little warm." Gemma stepped back and wrenched her tunic top over her head, standing before him, in a purple lacey bra and her trousers. She dropped the garment on the floor behind her. Saxon lowered his head and with his teeth, teased one of her nipples through its lacey cover, causing her to moan with exquisite pleasure.

This time, Saxon took the initiative. Grasping her hand, he pulled her from the room and down the passage leading to her bedroom. He kissed her again, holding her close so that the level of his desire for her was obvious. When she stroked his swollen member through the fabric of his jeans, he gasped aloud.

In wordless agreement, they slid out of their trousers and Gemma unhooked her bra and cast it aside. He breasts settled comfortably, though hardened and inviting his touch. Saxon scooped her up easily, and flung her onto the bed, joining her with a thigh pressed between hers as his hands roamed over her body. The violet aura still played on the periphery, highlighting their skin with an unusual luminosity.

He nibbled down the side of her neck, discovering erogenous zones she didn't know existed. She relished the sensation of his skin against hers, and the way he responded as she explored the areas of his body she could reach. Saxon eased a finger between the front of her panties and her skin, seeking and exploring the slit that lay beneath. Gemma gasped and bucked beneath him, knowing that her wetness signaled a need for more.

With a moan of desire, she raised her bottom and eased the panties from her legs. Taking the hint, Saxon likewise kicked off his jocks, allowing his cock to spring to unfettered attention. He grabbed a pillow and pushed it under her elevated buttocks, giving him better access to her nub of desire. With his tongue and his thumb, he brought her to a mind-blowing climax, as he watched with obvious satisfaction.

Reaching into the bedside drawer, Gemma extracted a small foil packet and handed it to him. "I don't want you to be left out of the fun."

"I won't be," he muttered as he sheathed himself and plunged into her moist and welcoming centre.

Sated, they lay side-by-side with legs still entwined.

"I never expected this as a result of my visit to town. You didn't predict this when reading my cards."

She smiled to herself. He clearly didn't remember. Gemma sensed a movement at the corner of her eye and knew a woman hovered in the shadows. She banished the vision with gratitude. This was neither the time or place for an observer. Besides, her work was done. Maretta, if that was her name, could rest easy. The person she hadn't read the cards for was herself. There was no need for that. She snuggled closer into Saxon's embrace. The thrumming she could hear settled to the level of a contented purr as she turned to face the tall, dark, handsome stranger in her bed. The Goddess moved in mysterious ways. Who knew that it would be for her?

***

Wild Card was first published in The Love Hexperts, Ballydoon Publishing, 2024, an anthology of stories all set in Leavenworth, WA, USA celebrating Halloween.

It is also an introduction to characters from the **Tales from Harrow** Series

Five Minutes of your time

Receiving a review from you would be so helpful in my journey as an author. You can do that by:

- posting on Facebook at https://www.facebook.com/EmilyHusseyAuthor/
- Posting on my website as https://emilyhussey.com.au

If you want to contact me direct, you can do that at emily@emilyhussey.com.au.
Subscribe to my newsletter at https://sendfox.com/emilyhussey.

Your comments will help me in providing a great story, and your reviews will be helpful to future readers.

Thank you

Emily Hussey

The Red Centre Series

Set against the breathtaking backdrop of Alice Springs and Australia's rugged heartland, *The Red Centre Series* follows the journeys of three very different women—each searching for purpose, healing, and love. In *The Red Heart*, pilot Kathy Sullivan finds turbulence both in the skies and on the ground. *Trust Your Heart* charts Sarah's path to new beginnings after loss, while *Follow Your Heart* peels back the layers of Melissa Gilbert's guarded heart. Rich with emotion, romance, and the raw beauty of the outback, this series celebrates resilience, second chances, and the power of choosing your own path.

Journey to the Heart is the Prequel to the series, and introduces all of the key characters.

*****

The Red Heart
Kathy Sullivan has no time for relationships. Securing a new job as company pilot in 1980's Alice Springs, she's focussed on developing her career. She didn't plan for the impact encounters with Alex Woodleigh would have on her. Each occasion results in conflict, so why does she feel the way she does?

When they are paired on a fire-spotting flight, the heat between them rises to a level Kathy never expected. When Alex is claimed by his attractive neighbour, Kathy feels she's been played for a fool. She vows to avoid him in future, if she can. In the face of disaster, Alex is forced to acknowledge the basis for his actions. Is it too late to convince Kathy his motivations are genuine?

Trust Your Heart
Embracing liquid refreshment more exuberantly than usual, Sarah falls off a table and into Joel's life. She introduces him to life in and around Alice Springs, but secrecy, for whatever reasons, gives rise to more problems than it hides. As water rises around him in the flooding Todd River, Joel is forced to question who he trusts. Is it too late for him to convince Sarah that with him, she has a chance for renewed happiness?

Follow Your Heart
Tragic events in her formative years colour a young woman's perceptions of her place in the world. Trust and commitment are not concepts she embraces. In a journey that takes her from a remote Australian station, to the high fashion world of Sydney and beyond, Melissa learns valuable lessons. She realises that family can be broader than you appreciate, and that she has choices to make in who she lets into her life, and who she loves.

***

Scan the QR Code below or type
https://kdp.amazon.com/en_US/series/WHJX7JW9BAD
into your browser.

Emily Hussey

Sandy Bay Series

The Australian coastal town of Sandy Bay is close enough to the Adelaide that its residents can access the city if they need to, but far enough away that they can ignore the city too. The town swells with visitors on weekends or during the holiday season, but at other times it's quiet and the locals like it like that.

In a small-town environment, everyone knows everyone else, and secrets can be difficult to keep. It's astonishing what things some people manage to hide for so long. Either in Sandy Bay, or the adjoining hub of Port Reilly, the unexpected may still surprise the most cynical resident.

No matter what the current crisis, the lure of the Bay and the pristine Australian beaches will continue to delight, not just the characters but the readers as well.

***

The Letters – a short story
Jacinta had loved spending holidays with her aunt in Pt Reilly. Her aunt was an artist, and they often spent time wandering up and down the coastal area, while Cynthia worked on her latest seascape and Jacinta swam or collected shells.

On arrival at the seaside cottage each year, she would check that nothing had changed. She found reassurance in the consistency of the things in the house, the times they shared together, and her aunt's unquestioned presence.

Except one day Cynthia wasn't there anymore, and Jacinta learned that the house, its contents, and its memories had been left to her. As she sorted through the last of her aunt's worldly possessions, she discovered the tragedy that had shaped the path of Cynthia's life.

Secrets in Sandy Bay—an introductory novella
It was late on a Friday afternoon, but was that any excuse? Property Manager Maddie's heart sinks when she realises she has given Alex Isherwood the wrong keys to his rental cottage. It's already dark, and the weather is foul and promising to get worse. There's no other option—she has to drive out to Seaspray Cottage and sort out this mess.

Give him the keys—that was all she had to do. So how was it that an hour later, she was sitting in front of an open fire, minus her own clothes, and sharing a meal with a man who didn't take 'No' for an answer? The tempest outside was nothing to the storm that was stirred up inside the cottage.

With a shared history in the town, they had a few things in common, but didn't know how much. It's amazing how tightly held some secrets can be, even in a small town where everyone knows everything.

Maddie's world disintegrates as the secrets of her past are revealed.

Escape to Sandy Bay
Alyssa needs to escape… from her job, her dreams, and her man. She flees to coastal Sandy Bay to lick her wounds.

The town of her childhood holidays provides a job and a place to stay.

Her new-found sanctuary is shattered when she learns of a controversial proposal that will change the face of the sea front forever. When she sees a man undertaking preliminary site investigations, Alyssa springs into action, determined to thwart the development.

Max is focused on caring for his young son and building the reputation of his business. He's not looking for trouble, but in the guise of a lawyer who is quick to react, trouble comes looking for him. She stirs the emotions in ways he didn't expect, but when she neglects his son, he's quick to lash out.

Leaving the past behind is not so easy, especially with unfinished business back in the city. Should she forgive and forget, or forge a new life so different to the one she'd always imagined? The responses of the men in her life influence the decision she needs to make, but which choice is the right one?

Return to Sandy Bay
Delia fled Sandy Bay with a secret she couldn't share. She left behind the carefree life that young people enjoyed in the coastal town. She also left behind the man she loved, resolutely forging a future and career in the city.

Work draws her back to the town in which she grew up, forcing her to confront her past and the people who shaped it. Some facts are easily manipulated, and not all actions are honourable. She can't hide the truth from Ben any longer, but there are surprises in store for both of them.

As one door in her life closes, another opens in the form of a new business opportunity, potentially bringing them closer together. She hasn't counted on the changing family dynamics when she made this move.

Will she give Ben a second chance, or will the fallout tear them apart?

Safe Harbour in Sandy Bay

When a yacht's electronics fail, corporate escapee Harley Mendelson is forced to dock in the close-knit fishing town of Sandy Bay. His gleaming vessel, Ocean Dream, carries not just his lifelong sailing ambitions, but the weight of a past he's left behind.

Local fisherman's daughter Lily Jardine has salt water in her veins and cynicism in her heart. To her, Harley is just another city slicker playing sailor—more suited to a kiddie pool than the open seas. But as engine repairs stretch from hours into days and beyond, she discovers depths in the quiet stranger that makes her question her hasty judgment.

As Sandy Bay's rustic charm begins to crack Harley's defensive shell, an unexpected connection sparks between two people from different social sets. Yet Harley knows he has no right to ask more of the free-spirited Lily. And she knows that dreamers who chase the horizon eventually sail away.

Romance in the Stone

Sometimes, the heart drops anchor when you least expect it—and the biggest adventures begin when you stop running from your past and finally find your way home.

A tale of second chances, sea-swept romance, and discovering that love might just be the best navigation system of all.

***

To access the series, scan the QR Code below, or type https://kdp.amazon.com/en_US/series/2MYW2V7A09 Q into your browser.

Tales from Harrow Series

The Harrow Series

Nestled in the misty folds of the Adelaide Hills, the village of Harrow hums with secrets. Here, the Goddess is honoured, ancient magic pulses beneath the soil, and the women of the Clan walk a fine line between light and shadow. But even in a place steeped in tradition, love has a mind—and magic—of its own.

From forbidden romances and elemental powers to dangerous enemies and soul-deep bonds, *The Harrow Series* weaves the stories of extraordinary women grappling with their gifts, their destinies, and the men who challenge their hearts. As dark forces gather and the past refuses to stay buried, each tale brings you deeper into a world where love may be fated, but survival is never guaranteed.

Enter Harrow—where magic is real, danger lurks in the most unexpected places, and every choice carries the weight of destiny.

Wild Spirit

In a world where destiny weaves its intricate tapestry, the lives of innocents hang in the balance. An unspeakable evil threatens their very existence. Bronwen, bound by an unyielding sense of duty to the Clan, confronts a heart-wrenching choice that could alter her future forever.

Safeguard her sister's unborn child means leaving behind
the man she loves.
Amidst the shadows of secrecy, Kieran embarks on a
relentless quest, to reclaim the woman stolen from his
grasp. Unexpected allies emerge, offering a glimmer of
hope in their battle against the curse imposed by a rival
Clan.
The price of one woman's sacrifice reverberates through
their lives, threatening to shatter the fragile equilibrium
they hold dear. Amidst swirling forces of fate, can love,
resilience, and the enduring power of unity prevail, or will
darkness claim their world forever?

Wild Destiny
A moonlit night, a country road, a man in a hurry.
From the moment Daniel runs his car into a ditch, to
the scene he encounters in a remote part of the bush,
he struggles to make sense of what is happening.

In a quiet country town, Cassie invokes the support of
the Goddess in controlling her fate. She is a woman on
a mission, goaded by the women of the Clan and
determined to control her own destiny.

Orchids have long been known as sensual flowers, and
when Cassie distils the tincture from the Musky
Caladenia Orchid, the effects are mind-blowing.
Daniel can attest to that.
The Goddess brought them together; evil nearly tore
them apart.

Wild Tempest

Angus Galbraith's vineyard is devastated by a storm, and only one person could be behind it—the disastrous woman from his past. After a painful marriage to Willow, Angus had sworn off relationships. But when vet nurse Elodie Emslie cares for an injured koala he found, he's drawn to her confidence and resilience.

Elodie's skills as an animal healer work wonders for the koala joey, and as the autumn festival approaches, she and Angus find themselves thrown together. However, Willow, Angus's powerful ex-wife, becomes aware of their connection and unleashes her jealousy. Despite this, Angus and Elodie's bond continues to strengthen.

When a fire breaks out in the vineyard stables, Elodie's life is put in danger. The situation takes a darker turn when they face a deadly threat on the road to Harrow. With Angus's life on the line, Elodie must act quickly to save him before it's too late. The night holds more than one unexpected twist.

Wild Fire

Evie's ambitions blaze as fiercely as her hidden powers. Desperate to escape her small town and the watchful eyes of her wiccan clan, she sets her sights on the dazzling lights of stardom. But the path to fame is fraught with danger, and Evie soon learns that some gifts come with a scorching price.
Enter Conor, a mysterious biker shrouded in leather and secrets. His timely advice becomes Evie's mantra, urging her to seize control of her destiny. Yet as Conor grapples with his own family demons, he finds himself

inexplicably drawn into Evie's orbit, forced to choose between his past and a future he never imagined.

Unaware of the true extent of her abilities, Evie's newfound independence leads her to clash with the formidable Redbank Clan. It's a decision that could reduce her Hollywood dreams to ashes. As the heat rises, Evie must master the fire within or risk being consumed by forces beyond her control.
Tales from Harrow, Book 3: Dive deeper into the seemingly ordinary village of Harrow, nestled in the Adelaide hills. Beneath its quaint exterior lies a simmering cauldron of wiccan magic, forbidden love, and age-old rivalries. In this world, even the smallest spark can ignite an inferno of consequences.

***

To explore this series, type https://kdp.amazon.com/en_US/series/M0PWH8QZ5CA Into your browser, or scan the QR Code below.

Author Emily Hussey

Having lived in several Australian states, Emily Hussey now resides in a coastal suburb in Adelaide. Her twenties were spent in Alice Springs, which became the setting for the Red Centre Series.

While there, she also obtained her private pilot's licence, providing the technical background for the aviation scenes.

Emily enjoys the short story format, and has been published in local anthologies. The genres range from crime to romance, with some contemporary fiction for good measure. Much of her writing takes place with a persistent black and white cat demanding her attention.

She was a marriage celebrant for 24 years, and has married couples in many different locations, ranging from private gardens, to beaches to caves or rural locations. Many of her clients remain friends to this day.

The bottom drawer is always full of outlines for future projects. So many ideas, so little time.

Scan the QR Code below to access contact points, or type the following links into your browser.

Website: http://emilyhussey.com.au,
Queries:
    http://emilyhussey.com.au/contact/.
Facebook:
    https://www.facebook.com/EmilyHusseyAuthor/
Email: emily@emilyhussey.com.au

Your reviews and feedback are welcomed.